STANISLAW LEM'S

THE SEVENTH VOYAGE

ADAPTED BY

JON J MUTH

TRANSLATED BY

MICHAEL KANDEL

graphix

AN IMPRINT OF

SCHOLASTIC

FOR STANISLAW LEM
AND FOR ALL THOSE WHO
LOVE HIS WRITING

Library of Congress Cataloging-in-Publication Data

Names: Muth, Jon J, adapter, illustrator. | Lem, Stanislaw. | Kandel, Michael, translator.
Title: The Seventh Voyage / by Stanislaw Lem ; illustrated by Jon J Muth ; translated by Michael Kandel.
Description: First edition. | New York, NY : Graphix, an imprint of Scholastic Inc., 2019. | Adapted from the short story
"The Seventh Voyage" by Stanislaw Lem, which appears in his collection "The Star Diaries." | Summary: In this graphic
adaptation of a story by Stanislaw Lem, a meteoroid damages astronaut and space traveler Ijon's spaceship,
and he finds himself caught in a time loop, contending with past and future versions of himself.

Identifiers: LCCN 2018058501 | ISBN 9780545004626 (paper over board : alk. paper)
Subjects: LCSH: Tichy, Ijon (Fictitious character—Comic books, strips, etc. | Tichy, Ijon (Fictitious character)—
Juvenile fiction. | Astronauts—Comic books, strips, etc. | Astronauts—Juvenile fiction. |
Time travel—Comic books, strips, etc. | Time travel—Juvenile fiction. | Science fiction. | Outer space—Comic books,
strips, etc. | Outer space—Juvenile fiction. | Graphic novels. | CYAC: Graphic novels. | Science fiction. | Astronauts—
Fiction. | Time travel—Fiction. | Outer space—Fiction. | LCGFT: Science fiction.
Classification: LCC PZ7.7.M95 Se 2019 | DDC 741.5/973--dc23

ISBN 978-0-545-00462-6

10 9 8 7 6 5 4 3 2 1   19 20 21 22 23

Jon J Muth created his artwork with watercolor and pencil.

Printed in Malaysia 108
First edition, October 2019
Edited by Dianne Hess
Book design by Phil Falco and Shivana Sookdeo
Lettering by E.K. Weaver
Creative Director: Phil Falco
Publisher: David Saylor

IJON TICHY'S NAME IS PRONOUNCED:

EE-yon TEE-khee

INTRODUCTION

It is with great joy and deep emotion that we offer the reader this illustrated account of Ijon Tichy's Seventh Voyage. This volume will be of particular interest to Tichyologists in that this is the first visual depiction to be retrieved with an intact on-board drawing computer. The R.MUTTH 5800, the entity responsible for the drawings herein, is a minor program with very limited capability, but we feel its illustrations may illuminate the events herein . . . somewhat.

As we know, photographs were outlawed in the early twenty-first century, after it was discovered they were completely unreliable sources of objective information. Photography's ethical downfall is recounted in numerous sociological and legal studies. It began with the digital manipulation used in motion picture production. As this technology became pervasive, the advent of the "smart" phone brought out the innately sly, unreliable, and sarcastic nature of the camera. Suspicions grew when simple snapshots from the family picnic had grandma in full scuba gear with a spear gun, and legitimate news outlets began offering photojournalistic accounts of farm animals running for public office.

Courts of law began using pencil drawings as the most truthful depiction of events. Security cameras were replaced by surly, non-communicative teens using art materials, and were later replaced with computers programmed to exhibit the same qualities. Computers were observed to render marginally better data, provided they were untainted with any functional intelligence.

Arranging for the publication of this visual depiction was by no means easy. The R.MUTTH 5800 found among the Tichy artifacts has been scrutinized by Tichographers from nine different institutes for Comparative Astro-Epistemological Studies as well as a gallery curator and an art critic from the *New York Times*. It has been found to suffer slightly from a Modernist aesthetic virus, but is generally believed to be honest if somewhat derivative in its representation of the events.

This particular R.MUTTH 5800 was prone to bouts of angst and childish behavior. Many back and forth negotiations between the publisher and the artsy-fartsy machine, as well as expensive lunches, gifts, and promises that the work would appear unaltered were proffered but produced few results. Even these promises didn't immediately assuage the fractious 5800's fears of overcommercialization of the work.

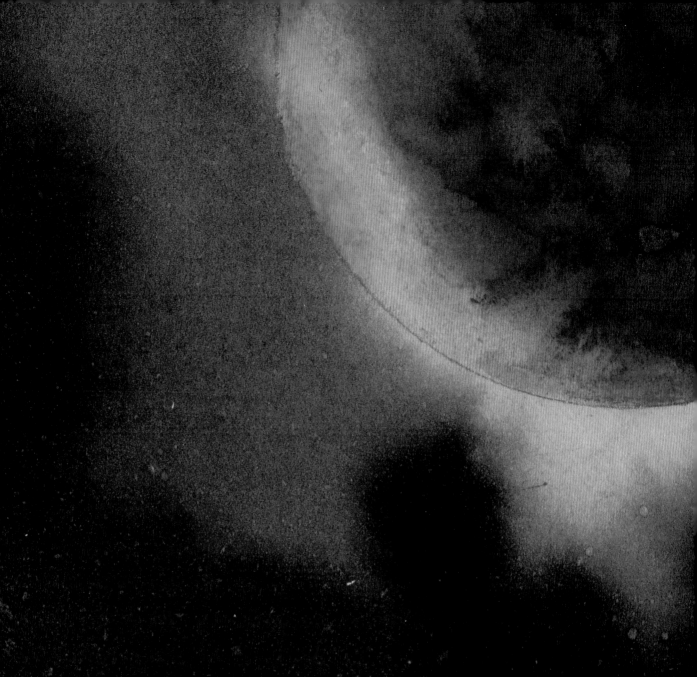

After some weeks of anguish and hurt feelings, wherein the computer began moping, wearing dark clothes, and acquired several new tattoos and piercings, an agreement was reached and the images from the Seventh Voyage were made available.

In conclusion, we hope the reader will find these renderings to possess some artistic or documentary value. As for the R.MUTTH 5800, it has since shaved its head and refuses to answer the door.

Professor Arthur Fraude

Acting Assistant to Professor A.S. Tarantoga, Department of Comparative Astrophotography on behalf of the Editorial Committee for the Publication of the Complete Works of Ijon Tichy

APRIL 1, 2319

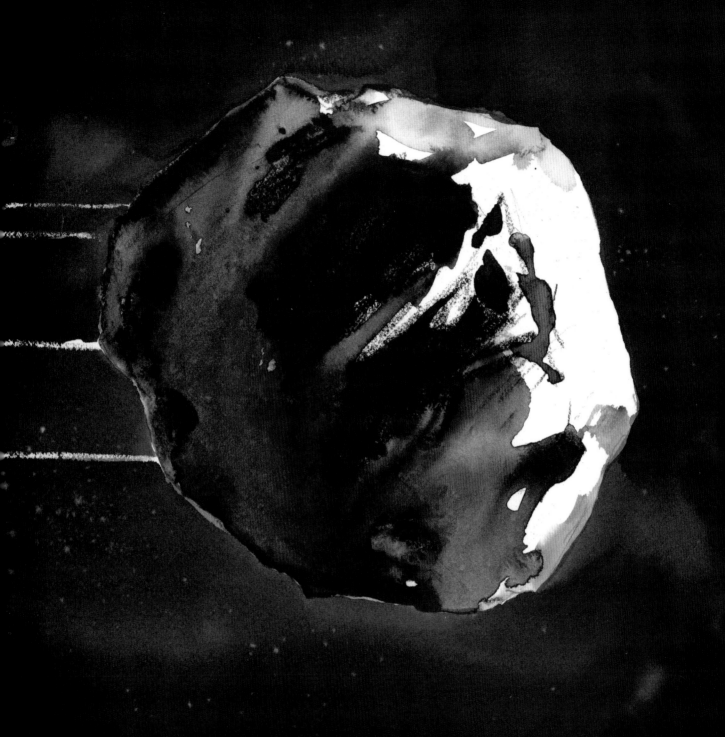

It was on a Monday, April 2nd...

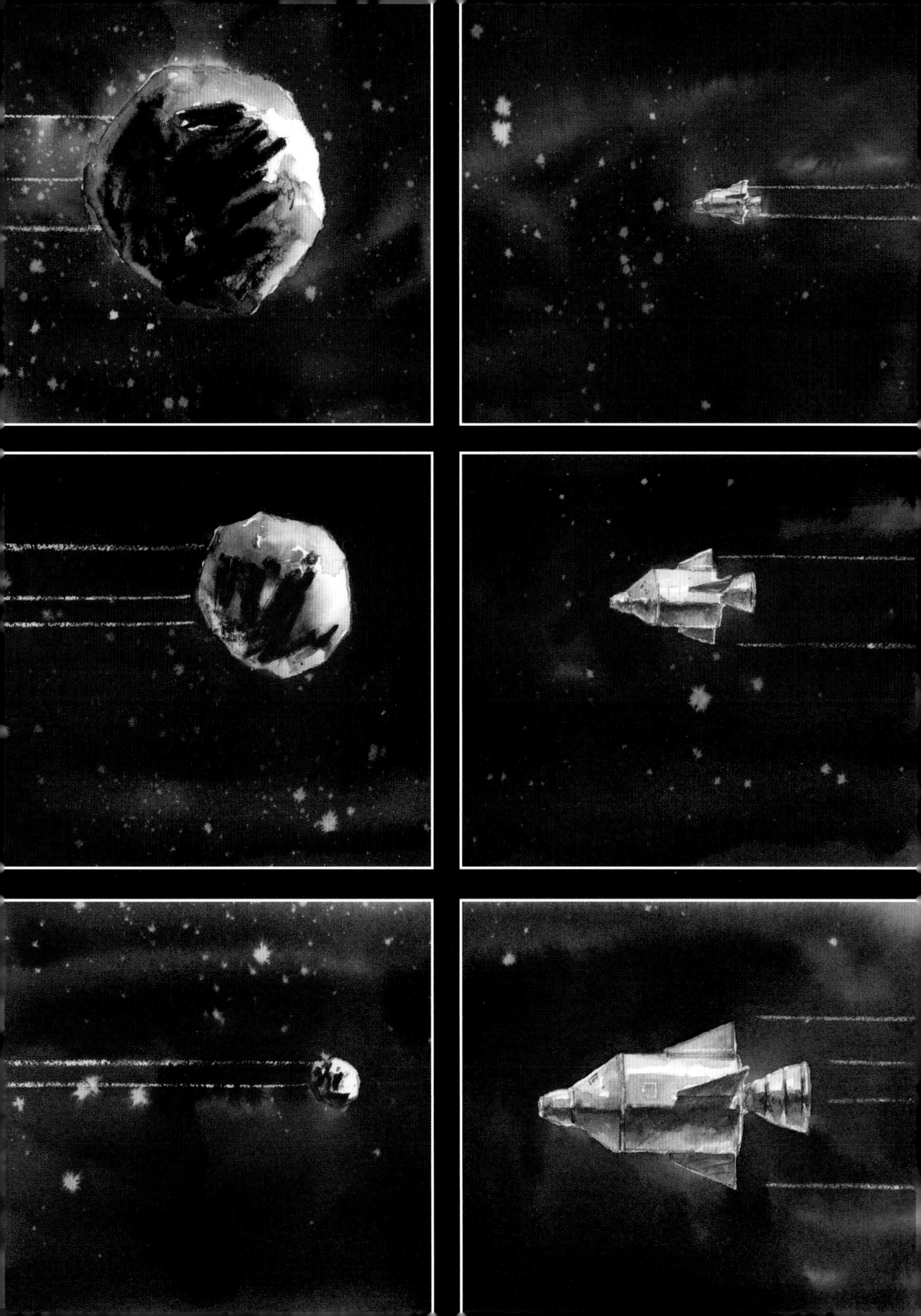

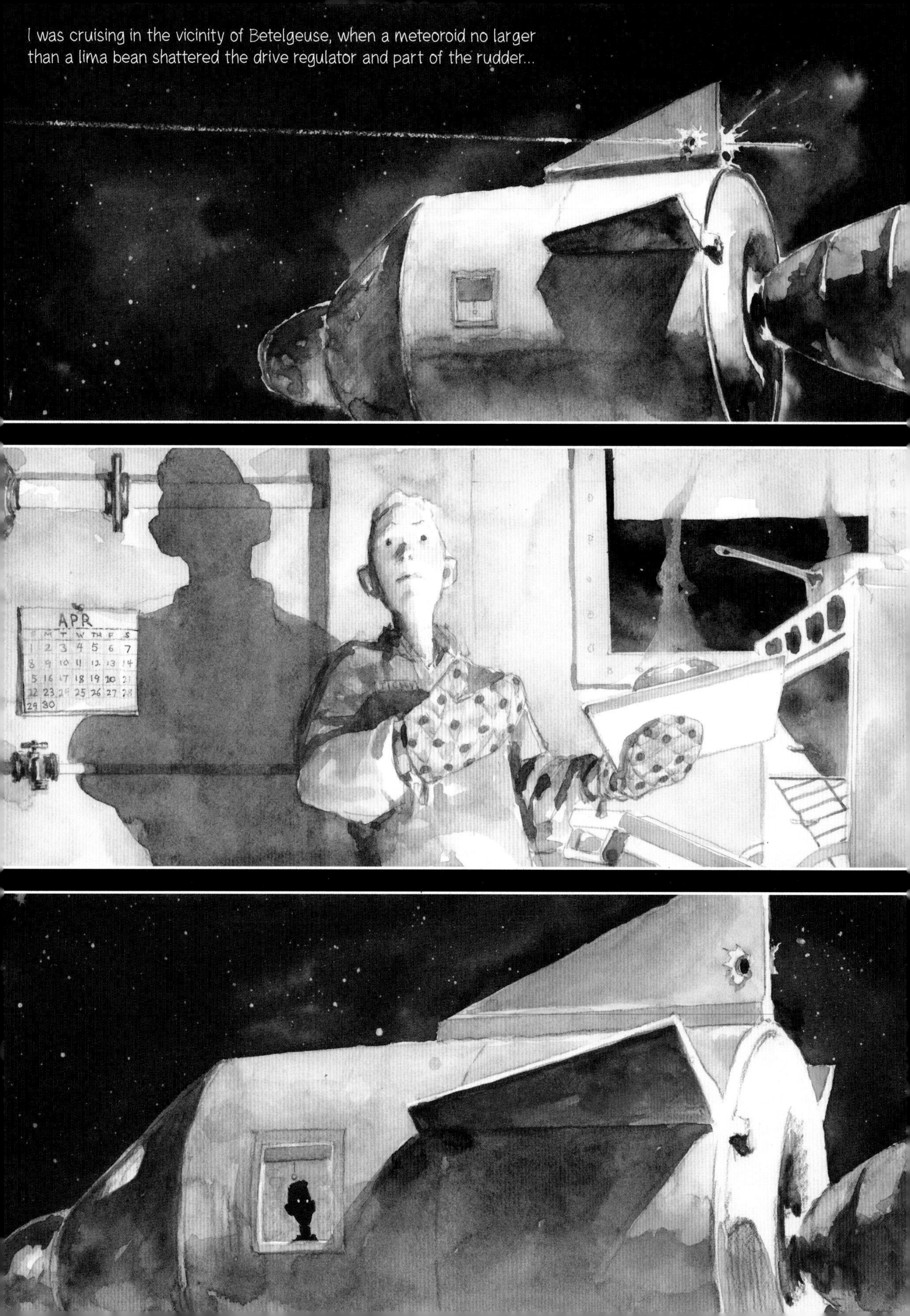
I was cruising in the vicinity of Betelgeuse, when a meteoroid no larger than a lima bean shattered the drive regulator and part of the rudder...
APR

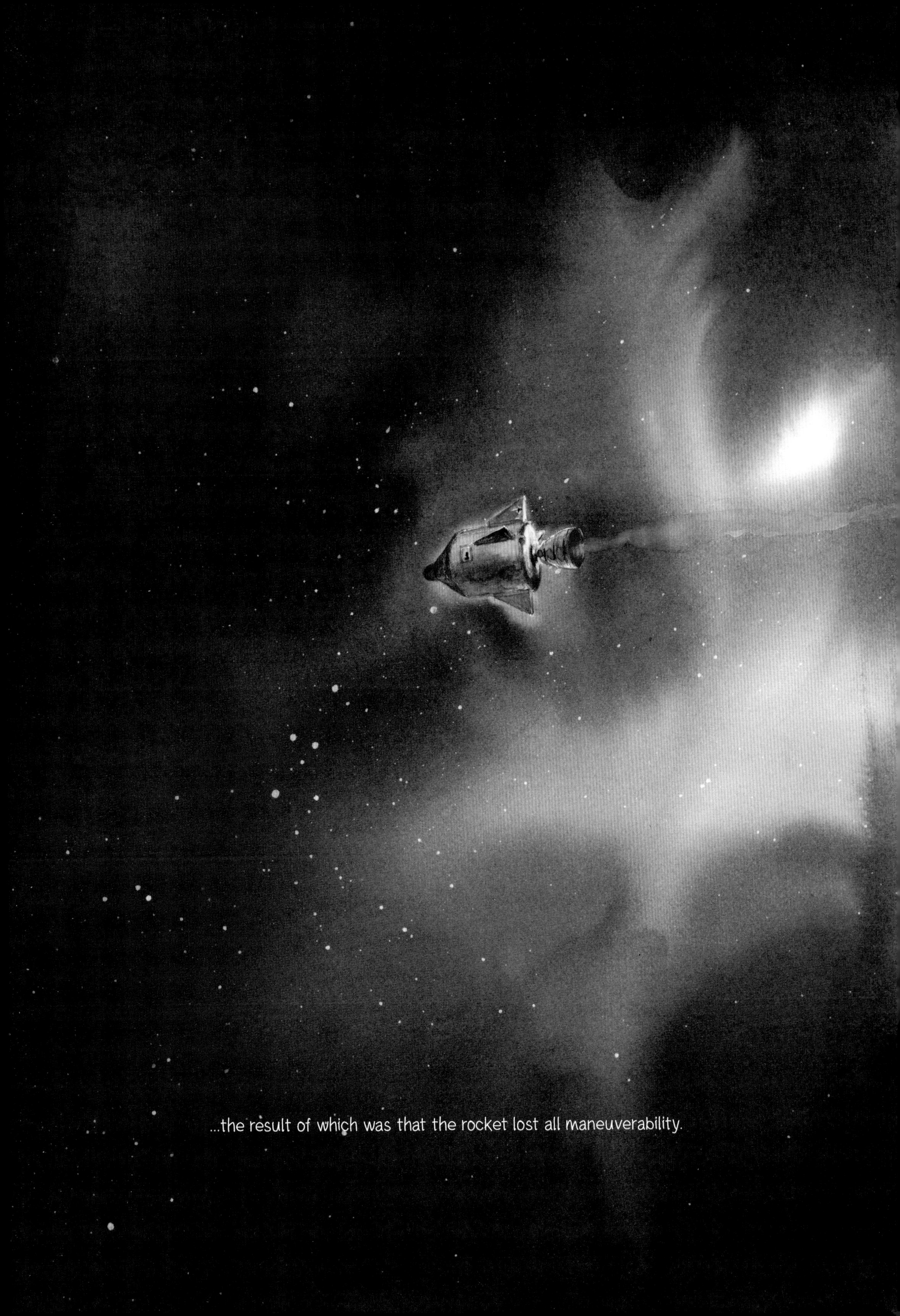
...the result of which was that the rocket lost all maneuverability.

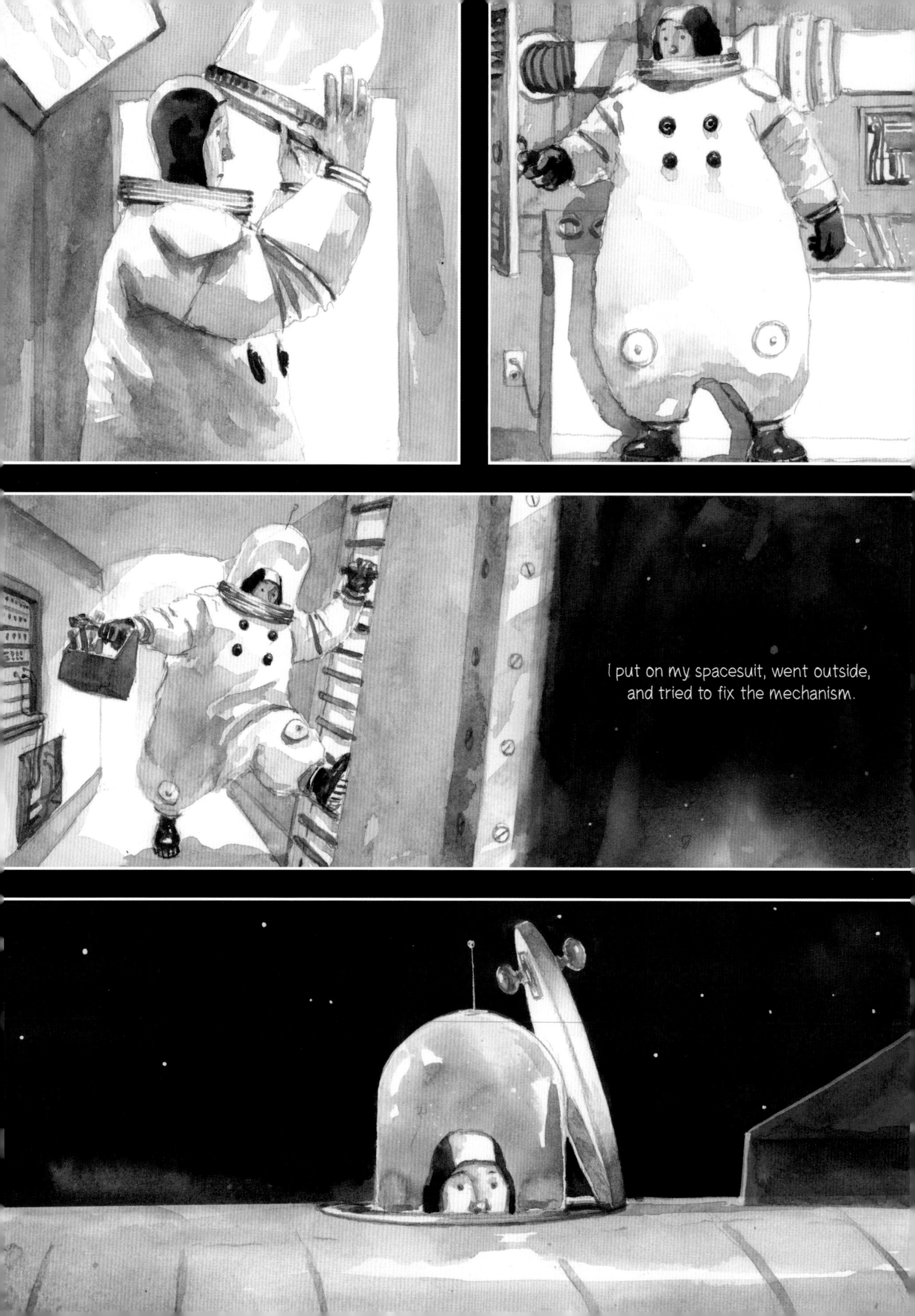
I put on my spacesuit, went outside, and tried to fix the mechanism.

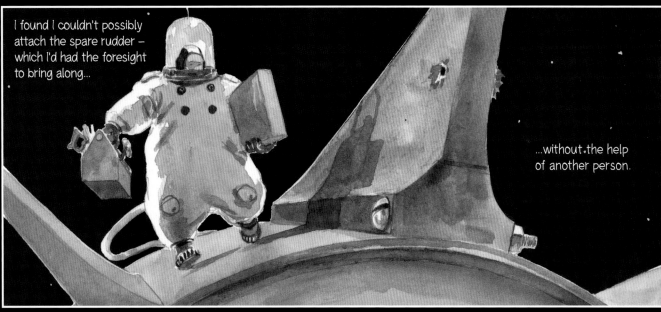

I found I couldn't possibly attach the spare rudder – which I'd had the foresight to bring along...

...without the help of another person.

The constructors had foolishly designed the rocket in such a way that it took one person to hold the head of the bolt in place with a wrench...

...and another to tighten the nut.

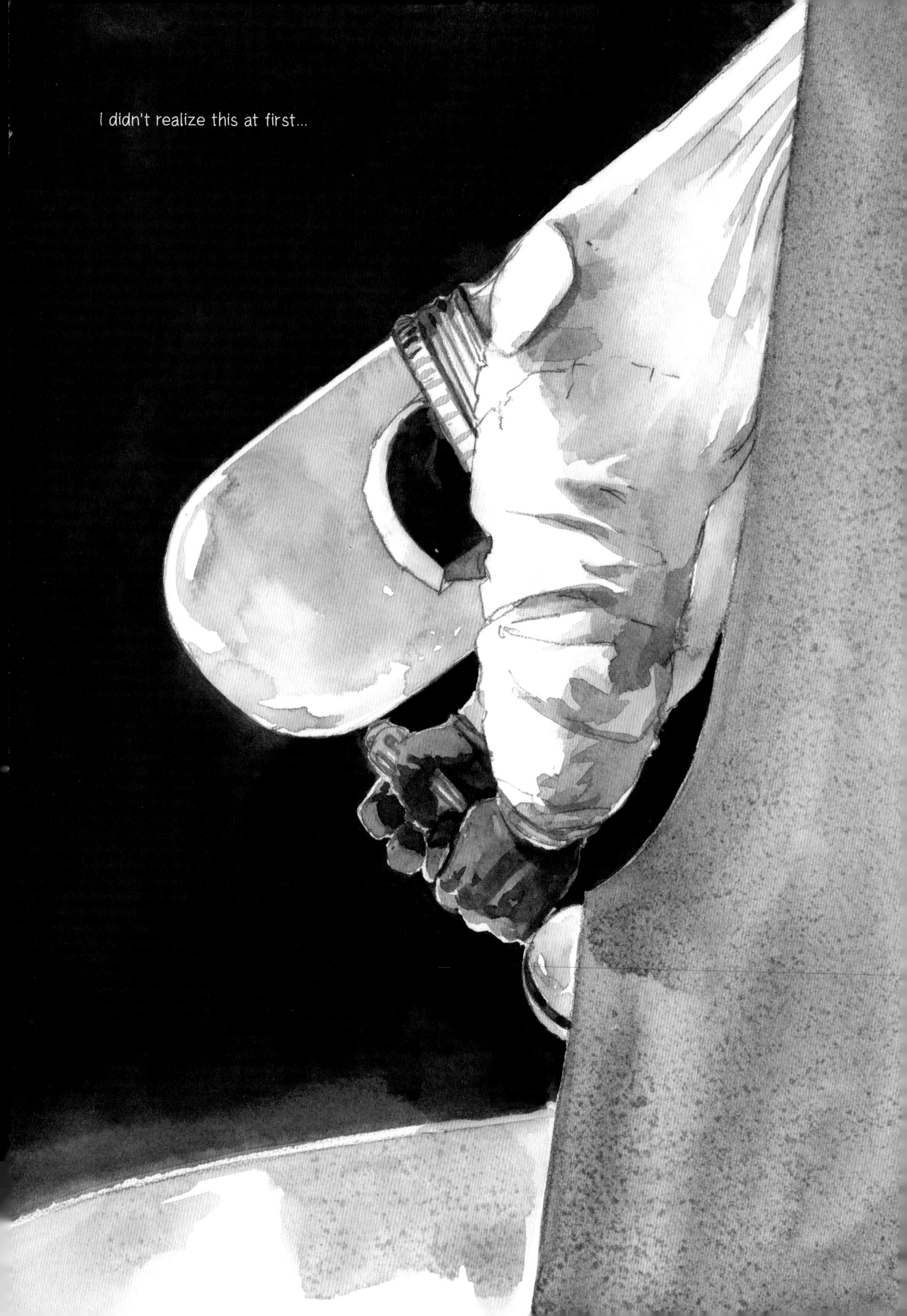
I didn't realize this at first...

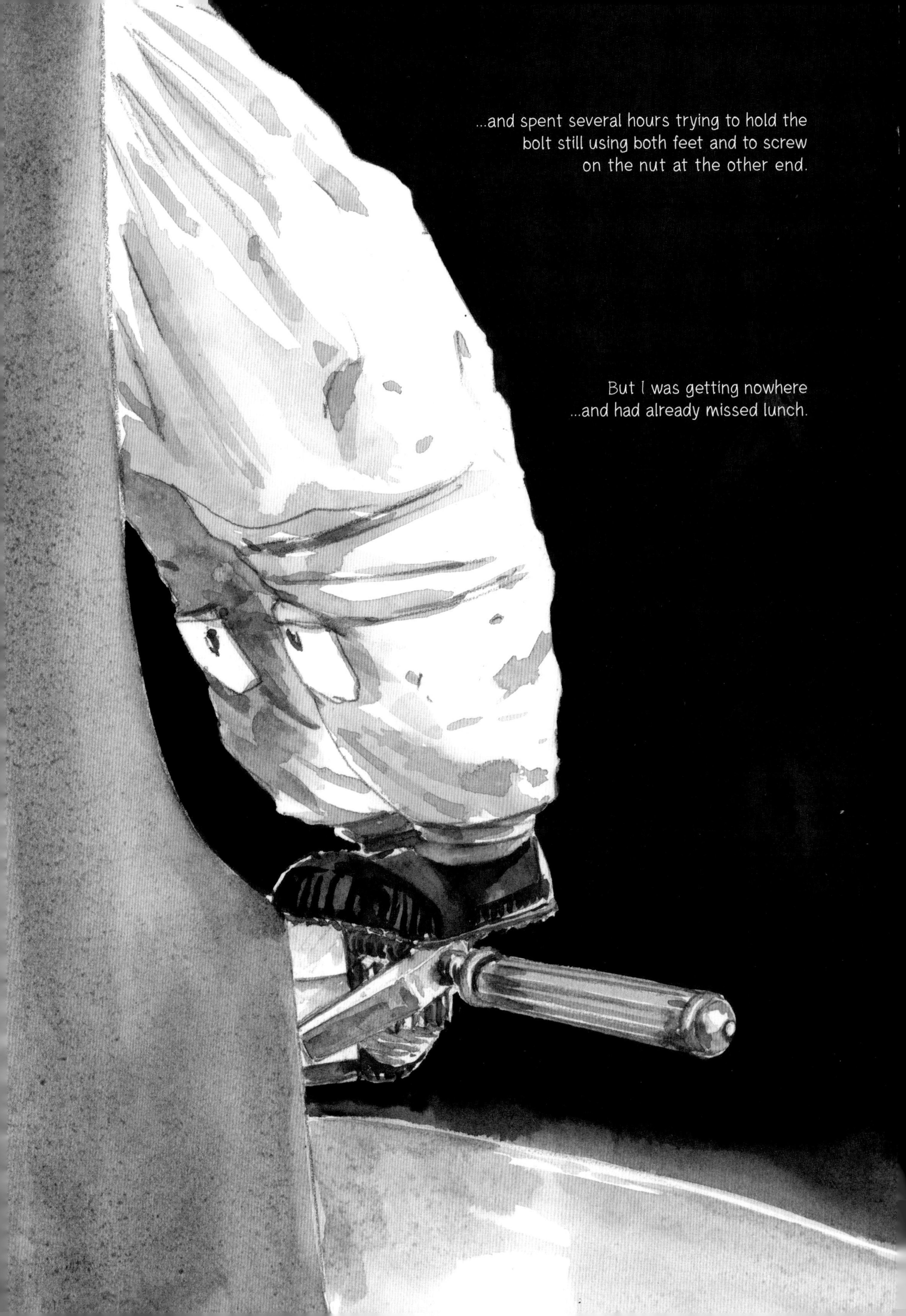
...and spent several hours trying to hold the bolt still using both feet and to screw on the nut at the other end.
But I was getting nowhere ...and had already missed lunch.

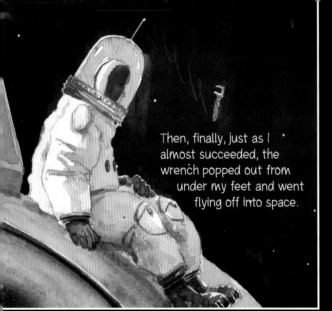

Then, finally, just as I almost succeeded, the wrench popped out from under my feet and went flying off into space.

After a while the wrench returned in an elongated ellipse, but though it had now become a satellite of the rocket, it never got close enough for me to retrieve it.

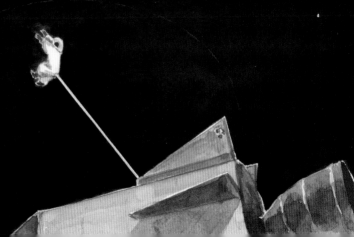

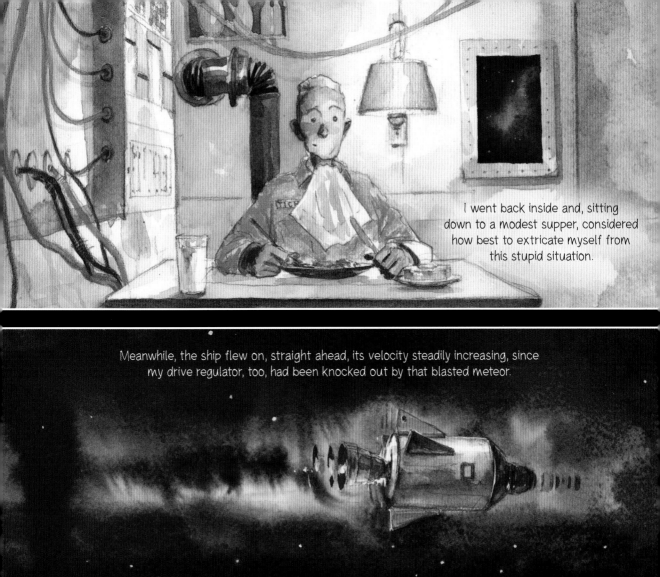

I went back inside and, sitting down to a modest supper, considered how best to extricate myself from this stupid situation.

Meanwhile, the ship flew on, straight ahead, its velocity steadily increasing, since my drive regulator, too, had been knocked out by that blasted meteor.

It's true there were no heavenly bodies on course, but this headlong flight could hardly continue indefinitely.

For a while I contained my anger, but then discovered, when starting to wash the dishes, that the now-overheated atomic pile had ruined my very best cut of sirloin.

(I'd been keeping it in the freezer for Sunday.)

I momentarily lost my usually level head, burst into a volley of the vilest oaths, and smashed a few plates.

This did give me a certain satisfaction...

...but it was hardly practical.

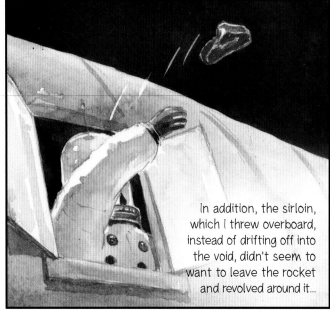

In addition, the sirloin, which I threw overboard, instead of drifting off into the void, didn't seem to want to leave the rocket and revolved around it...

...becoming a second artificial satellite, which produced a brief eclipse of the sun every eleven minutes and four seconds.

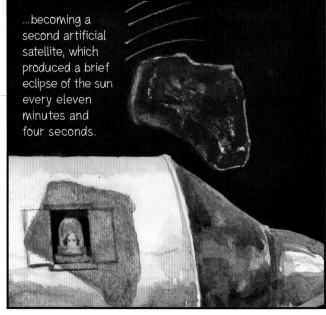

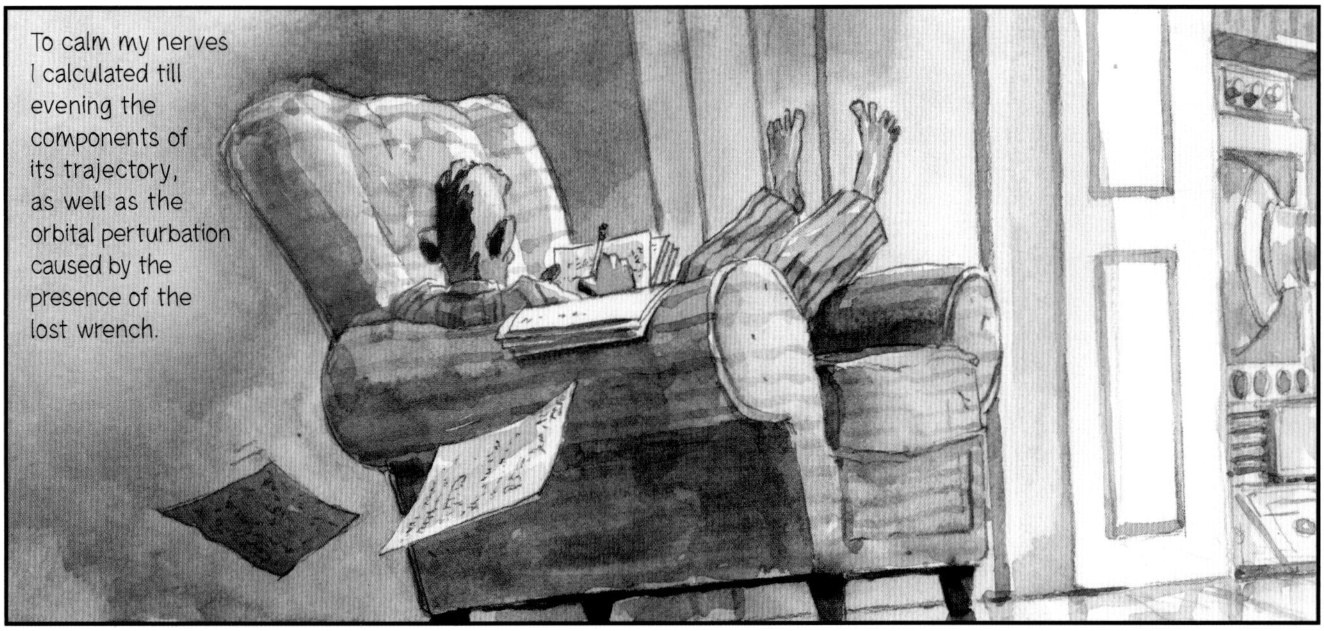
To calm my nerves I calculated till evening the components of its trajectory, as well as the orbital perturbation caused by the presence of the lost wrench.

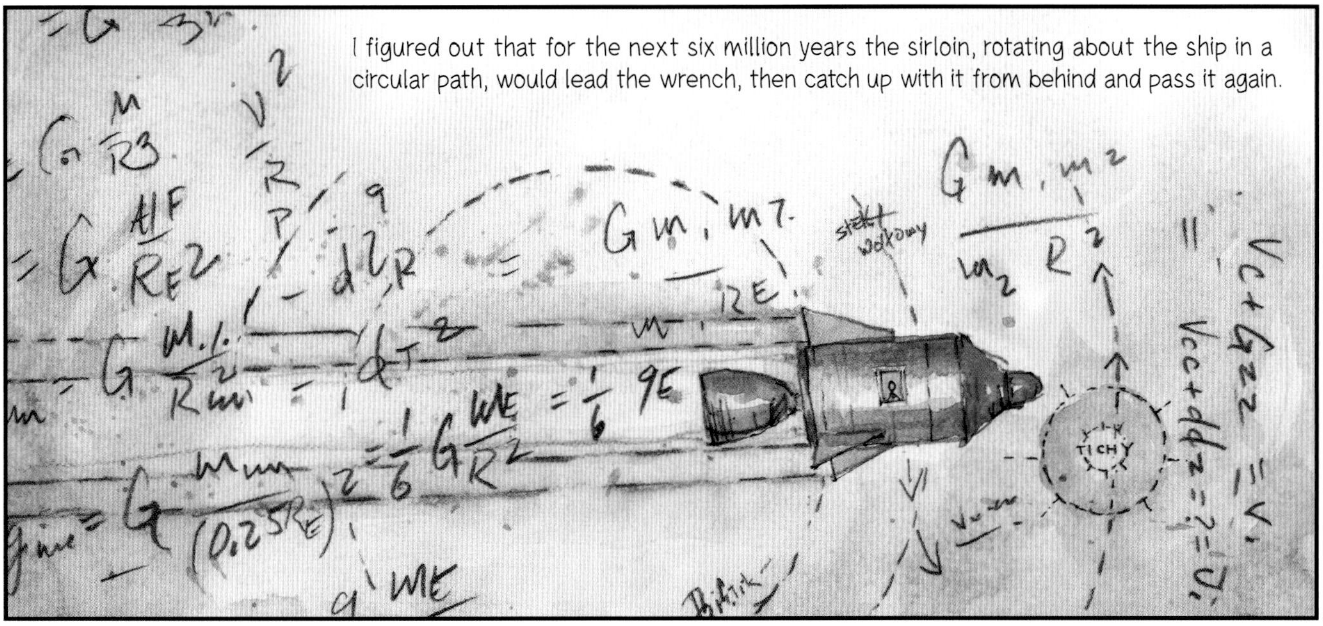
I figured out that for the next six million years the sirloin, rotating about the ship in a circular path, would lead the wrench, then catch up with it from behind and pass it again.
TICHY

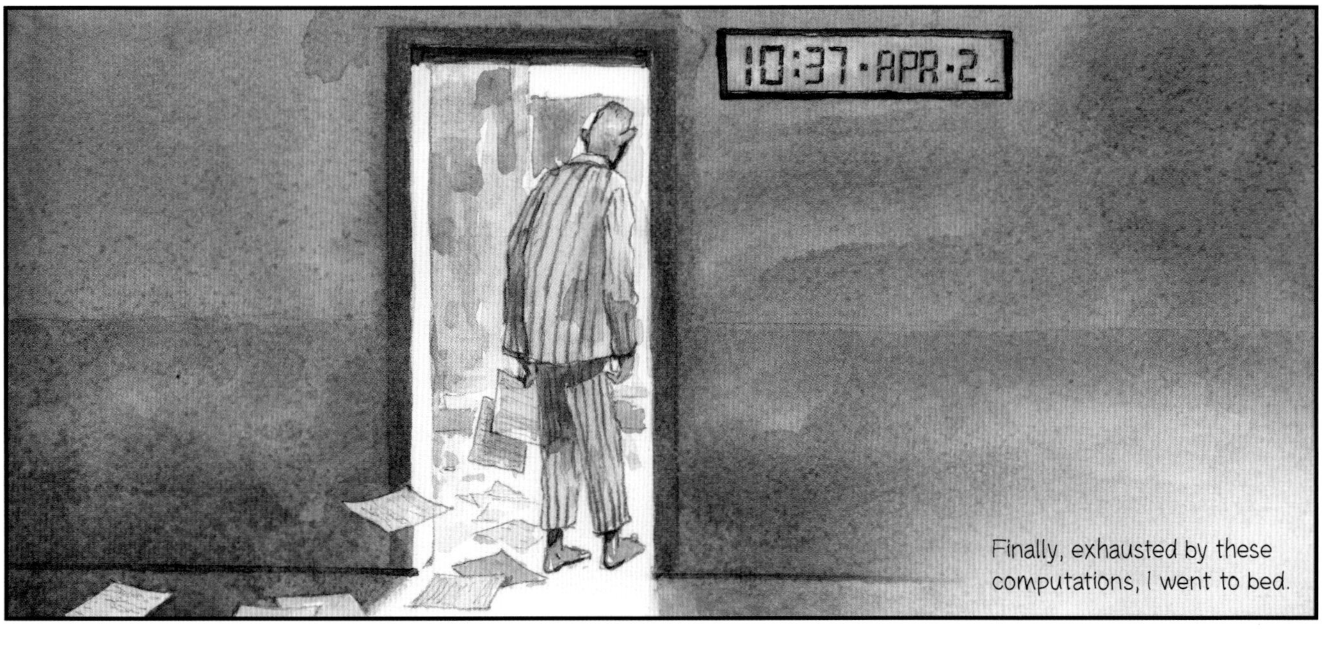
10:37 · APR · 2
Finally, exhausted by these computations, I went to bed.

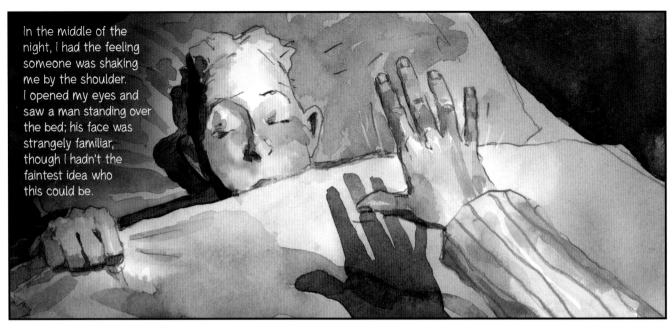

In the middle of the night, I had the feeling someone was shaking me by the shoulder. I opened my eyes and saw a man standing over the bed; his face was strangely familiar, though I hadn't the faintest idea who this could be.

Get up and take the pliers, we're going out and screwing on the rudder bolts.

First of all, your manner is somewhat unceremonious, and we haven't even been introduced, and secondly, I know for a fact that you aren't there.

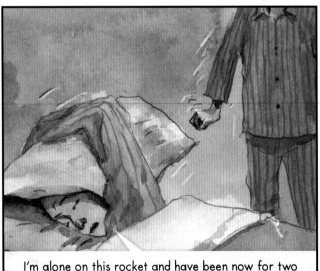

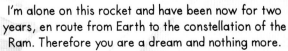

I'm alone on this rocket and have been now for two years, en route from Earth to the constellation of the Ram. Therefore you are a dream and nothing more.

However, he continued to shake me, repeating that I should go with him at once and get the tools.

This is idiotic.
This dream argument could
very well wake me up, and I know
from experience the difficulty I will
have getting back to sleep.

Look, I'm not going anywhere.
There's no point in it. A bolt
tightened in a dream won't
change things as they are
in the sober light of day.

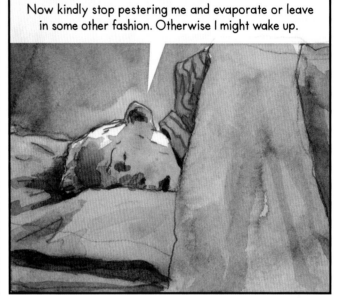

Now kindly stop pestering me and evaporate or leave
in some other fashion. Otherwise I might wake up.

But you *are* awake, word of honor!
Don't you recognize me?

Look here!

And saying this, the stubborn apparition pointed to the hourglass-shaped birthmark on his left buttock. Instinctively I clutched my own bottom, for yes, I had a birthmark, exactly the same, and in that very place.

Suddenly I realized why this phantom reminded me of someone I knew: He was the spitting image of myself.

Leave me alone, for heaven's sake!

And if you are me, then fine, we needn't stand on ceremony, but it only proves you don't exist.

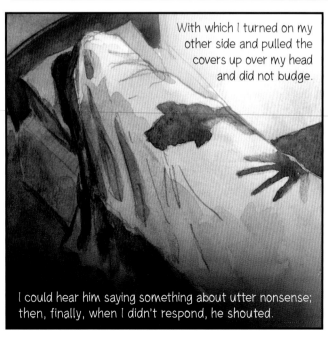

With which I turned on my other side and pulled the covers up over my head and did not budge.

I could hear him saying something about utter nonsense; then, finally, when I didn't respond, he shouted.

YOU'LL REGRET THIS, KNUCKLEHEAD. AND YOU'LL FIND OUT, TOO LATE, THAT THIS WAS NOT A DREAM!

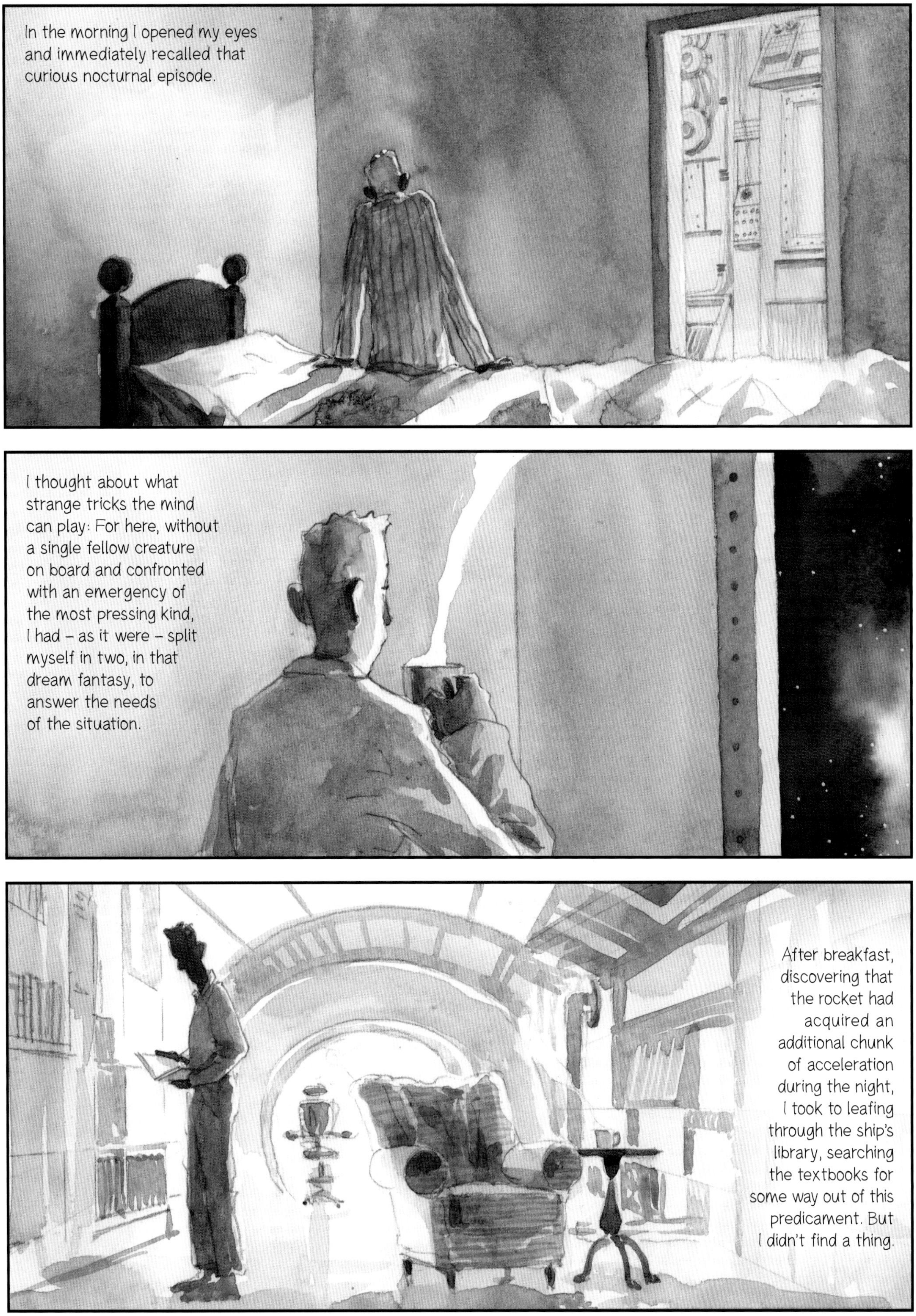
In the morning I opened my eyes and immediately recalled that curious nocturnal episode.
I thought about what strange tricks the mind can play: For here, without a single fellow creature on board and confronted with an emergency of the most pressing kind, I had – as it were – split myself in two, in that dream fantasy, to answer the needs of the situation.
After breakfast, discovering that the rocket had acquired an additional chunk of acceleration during the night, I took to leafing through the ship's library, searching the textbooks for some way out of this predicament. But I didn't find a thing.

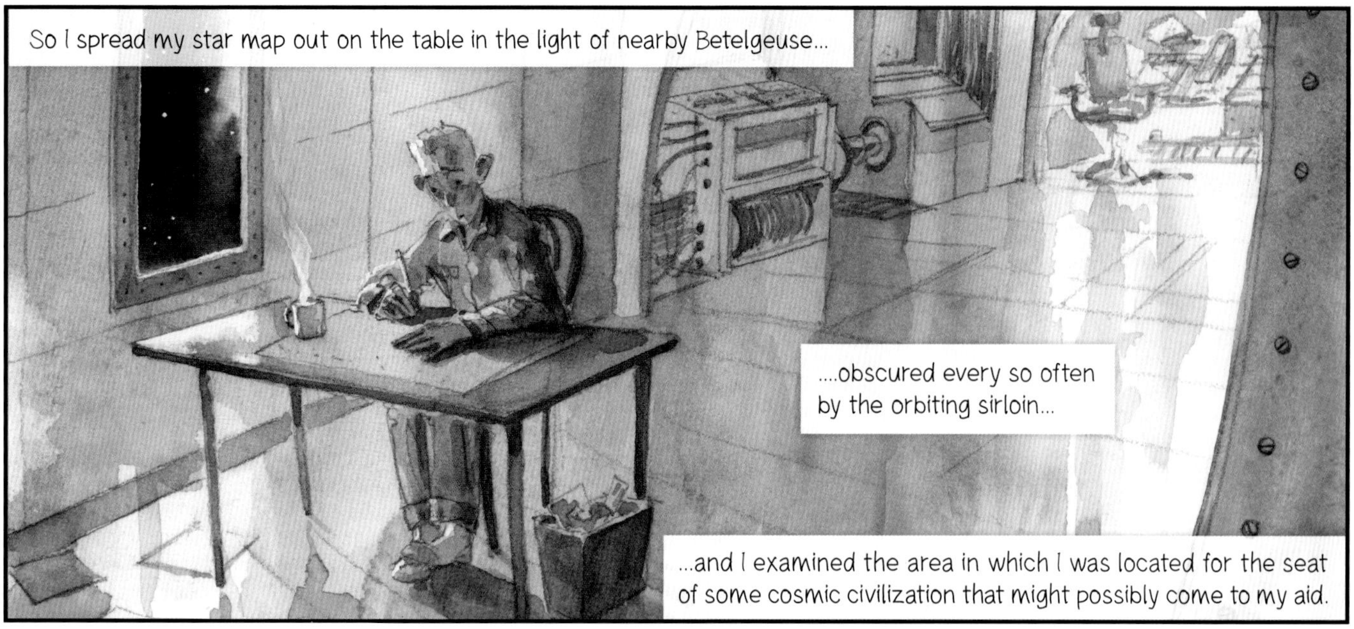
So I spread my star map out on the table in the light of nearby Betelgeuse...
....obscured every so often by the orbiting sirloin...
...and I examined the area in which I was located for the seat of some cosmic civilization that might possibly come to my aid.

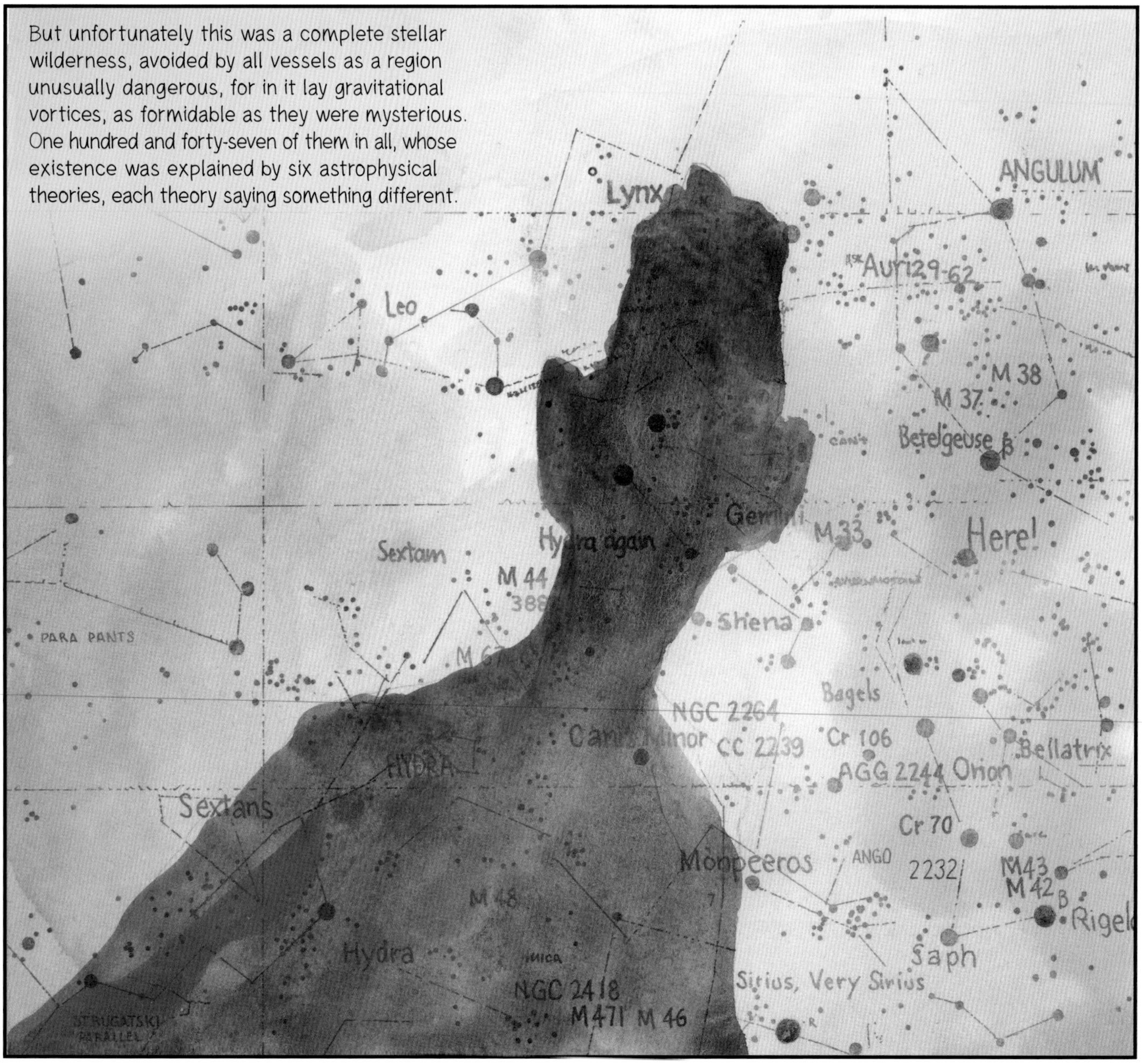
But unfortunately this was a complete stellar wilderness, avoided by all vessels as a region unusually dangerous, for in it lay gravitational vortices, as formidable as they were mysterious. One hundred and forty-seven of them in all, whose existence was explained by six astrophysical theories, each theory saying something different.
Lynx
ANGULUM
Leo
M 38
M 37
Betelgeuse
Here!
Sextam
M 44
PARA PANTS
Shiena
Bagels
NGC 2264
CC 2239
Cr 106
AGG 2244 Orion
Bellatrix
HYDRA
Sextans
Cr 70
ANGO
2232
M43
M42
Rigel
Hydra
Saph
Sirius, Very Sirius
NGC 2418
M471 M 46

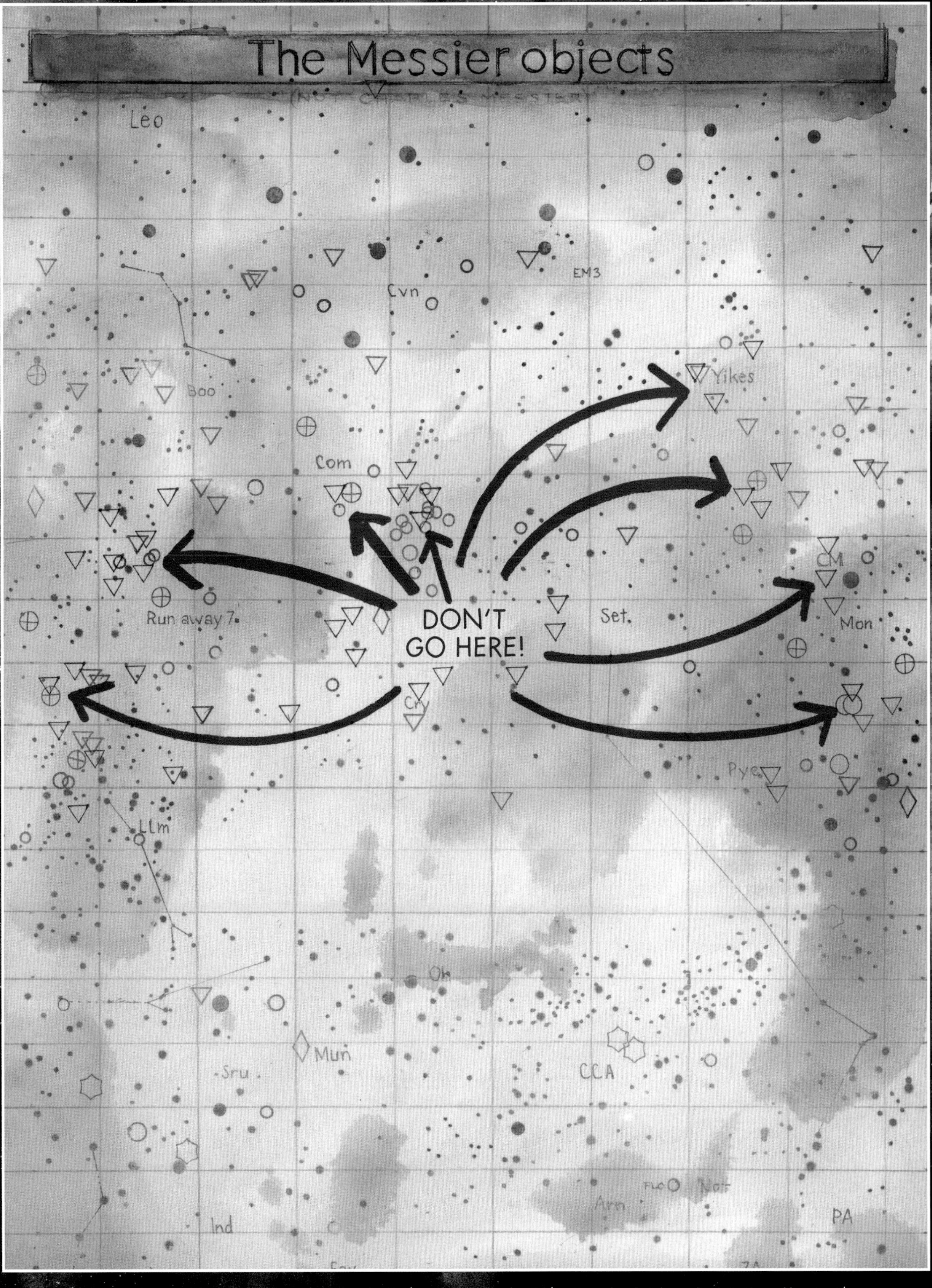
The Messier objects
(NOT CHARLES MESSIER)
Leo
Cvn
EM3
Boo
Yikes
Com
Run away 7
DON'T GO HERE!
Set.
CM
Mon
Cry
Pye
Llm
Oh
Mun
Sru
CCA
Arn
Ind
PA

The cosmonautical almanac warned of them, in view of the incalculable relativistic effects that passage through a vortex could bring about . . . particularly when traveling at high velocities.

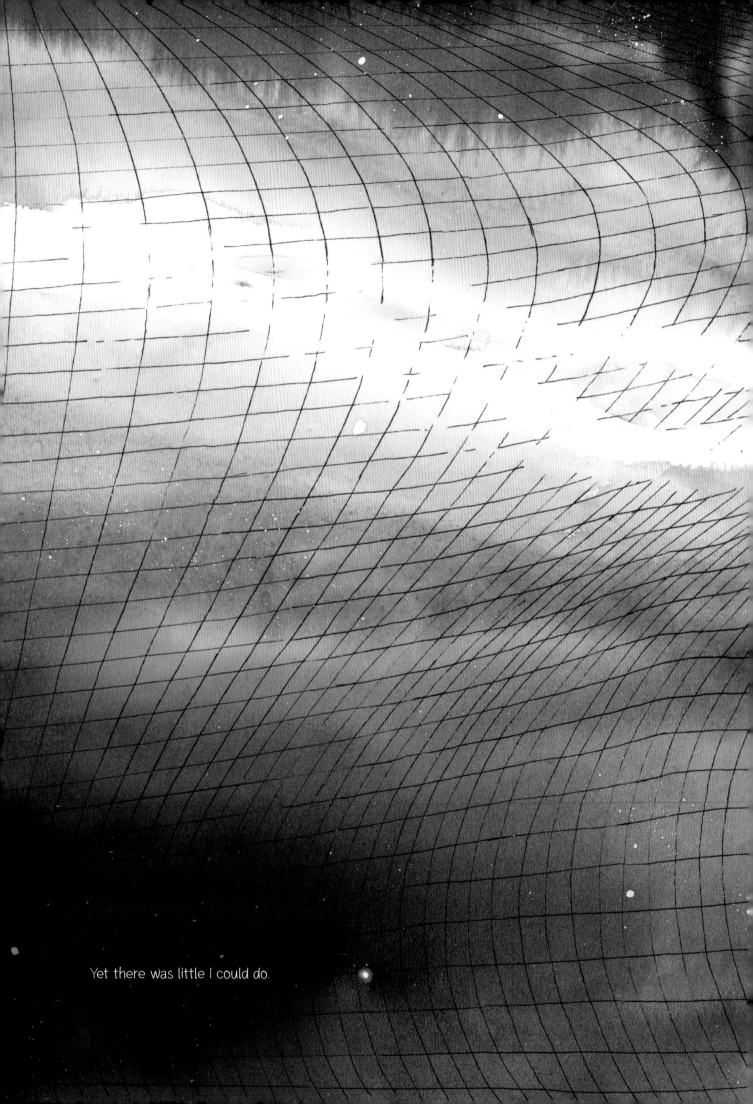

Yet there was little I could do.

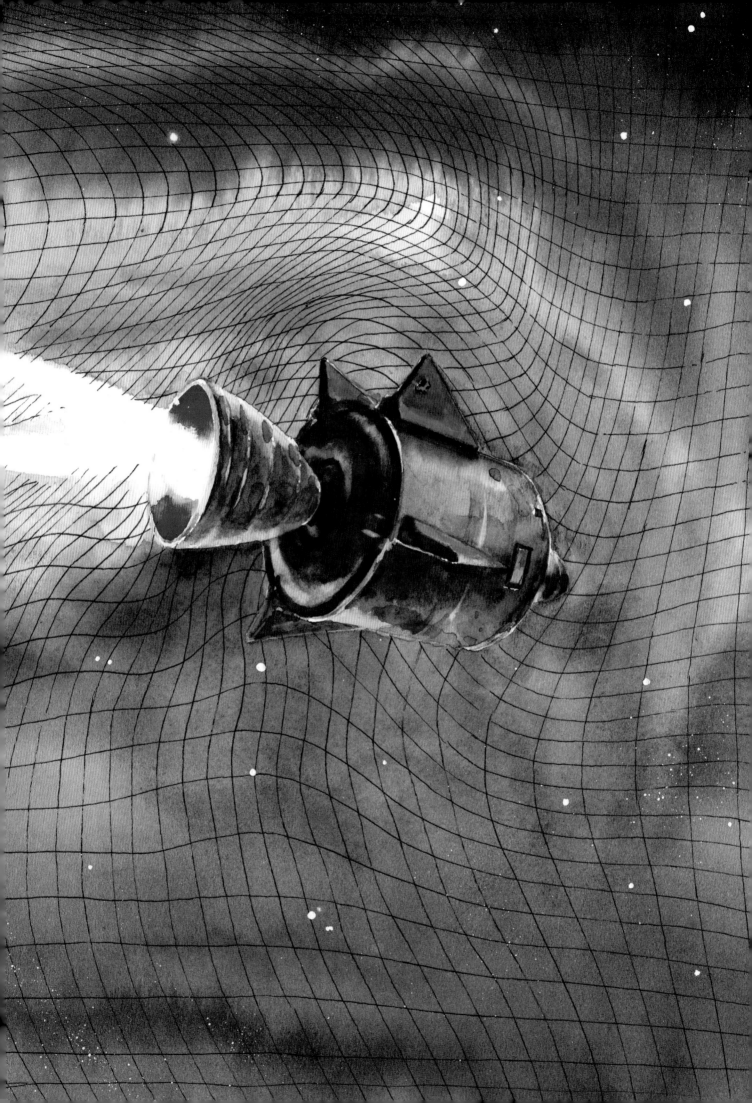

According to my calculations, I would be making contact with the edge of the first vortex at around eleven...

....and therefore hurriedly prepared lunch, not wanting to face the danger on an empty stomach.

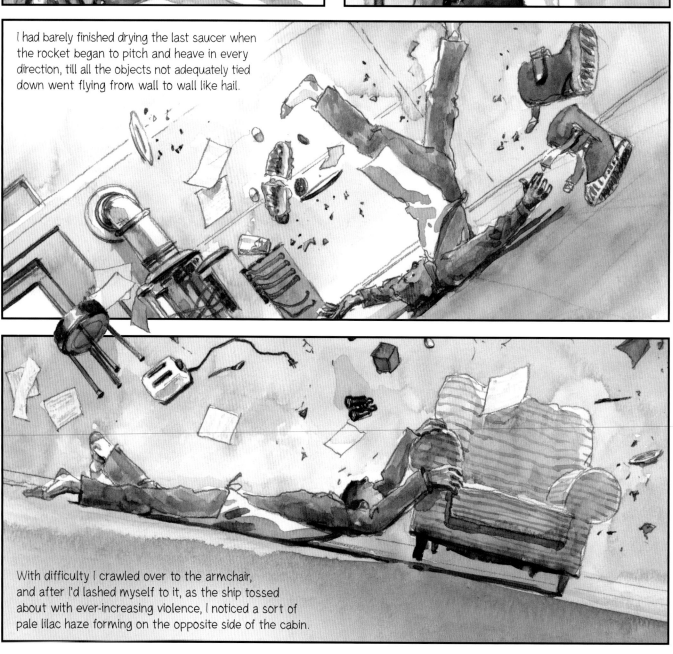

I had barely finished drying the last saucer when the rocket began to pitch and heave in every direction, till all the objects not adequately tied down went flying from wall to wall like hail.

With difficulty I crawled over to the armchair, and after I'd lashed myself to it, as the ship tossed about with ever-increasing violence, I noticed a sort of pale lilac haze forming on the opposite side of the cabin.

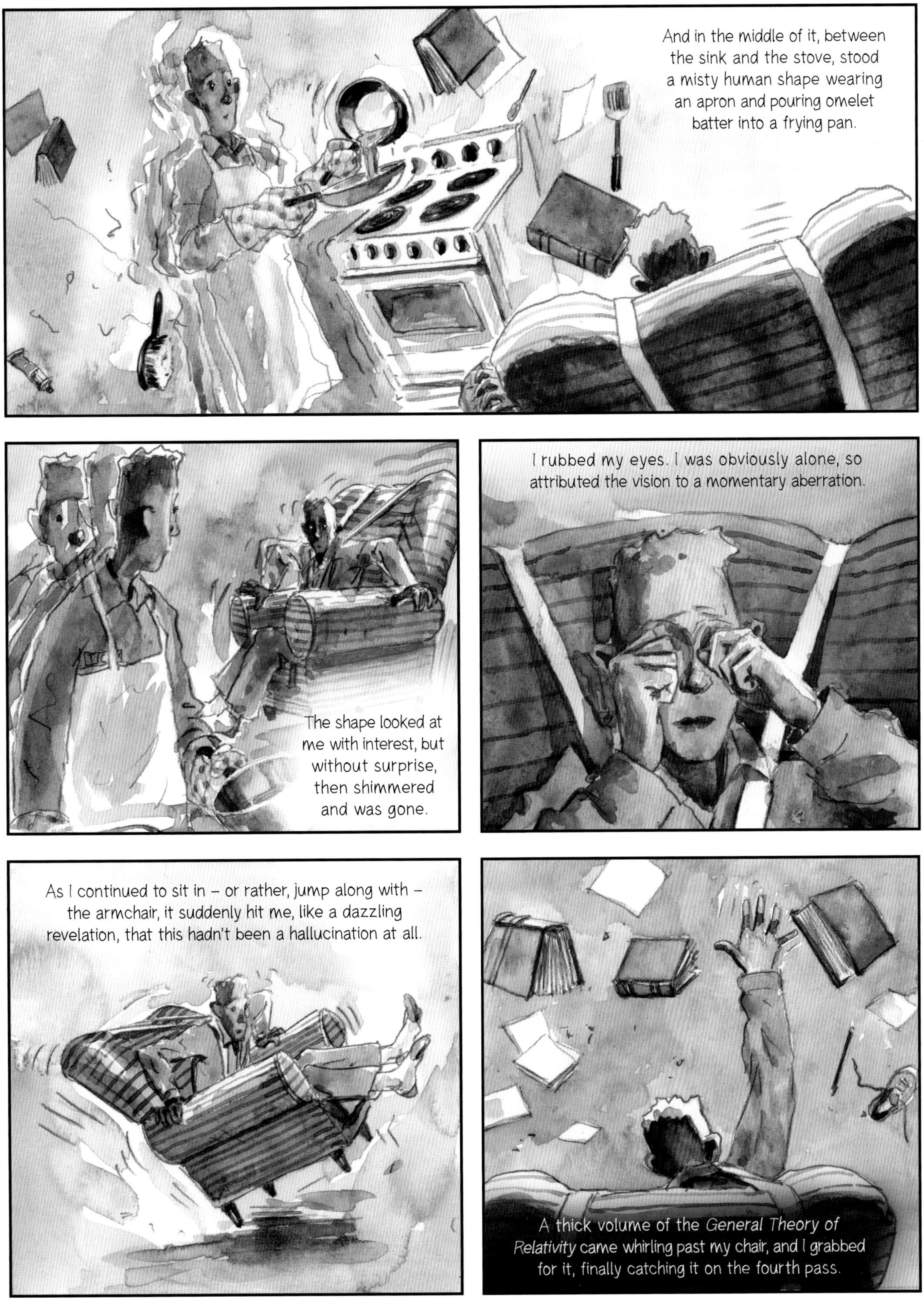
And in the middle of it, between the sink and the stove, stood a misty human shape wearing an apron and pouring omelet batter into a frying pan.
The shape looked at me with interest, but without surprise, then shimmered and was gone.
I rubbed my eyes. I was obviously alone, so attributed the vision to a momentary aberration.
As I continued to sit in – or rather, jump along with – the armchair, it suddenly hit me, like a dazzling revelation, that this hadn't been a hallucination at all.
A thick volume of the *General Theory of Relativity* came whirling past my chair, and I grabbed for it, finally catching it on the fourth pass.

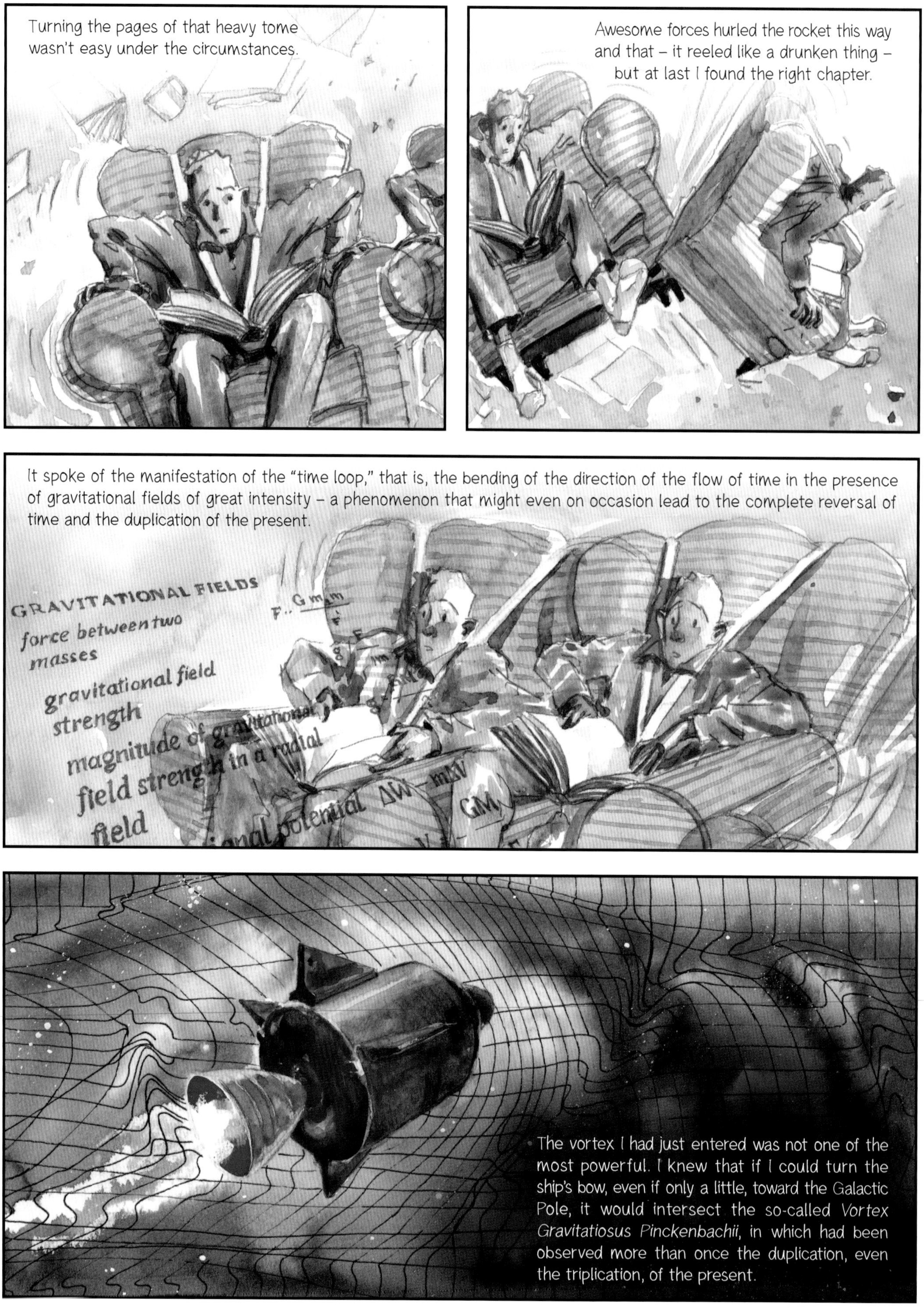
Turning the pages of that heavy tome wasn't easy under the circumstances.
Awesome forces hurled the rocket this way and that – it reeled like a drunken thing – but at last I found the right chapter.
It spoke of the manifestation of the "time loop," that is, the bending of the direction of the flow of time in the presence of gravitational fields of great intensity – a phenomenon that might even on occasion lead to the complete reversal of time and the duplication of the present.
GRAVITATIONAL FIELDS
force between two masses
gravitational field strength
The vortex I had just entered was not one of the most powerful. I knew that if I could turn the ship's bow, even if only a little, toward the Galactic Pole, it would intersect the so-called *Vortex Gravitatiosus Pinckenbachii*, in which had been observed more than once the duplication, even the triplication, of the present.

True, the controls were out, but I went down to the engine room and fiddled with the instruments for so long that I actually managed to produce a slight deflection of the rocket toward the Galactic Pole. This took several hours.

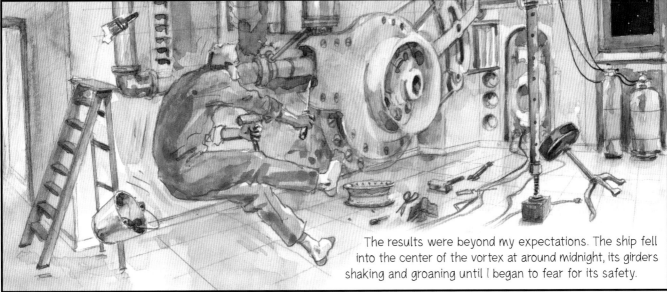

The results were beyond my expectations. The ship fell into the center of the vortex at around midnight, its girders shaking and groaning until I began to fear for its safety.

But it emerged from this ordeal whole and once again was wrapped in the lifeless arms of cosmic silence, whereupon I left the engine room and put on my pajamas...

...only to see myself sound asleep in bed.

I realized at once that this was I of the previous day, that is, from Monday night.

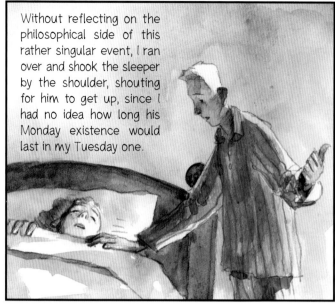

Without reflecting on the philosophical side of this rather singular event, I ran over and shook the sleeper by the shoulder, shouting for him to get up, since I had no idea how long his Monday existence would last in my Tuesday one.

It was imperative we go outside and fix the rudder as quickly as possible, together.

But the sleeper merely opened one eye and told me that not only was I rude, but didn't exist, being a figment of his dream and nothing more.

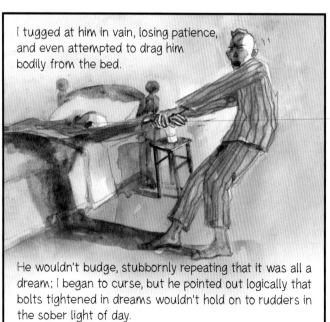

I tugged at him in vain, losing patience, and even attempted to drag him bodily from the bed.

He wouldn't budge, stubbornly repeating that it was all a dream; I began to curse, but he pointed out logically that bolts tightened in dreams wouldn't hold on to rudders in the sober light of day.

I gave my word of honor that he was mistaken, I pleaded and swore in turn, to no avail – even the birthmark did not convince him. He turned his back to me and started snoring.

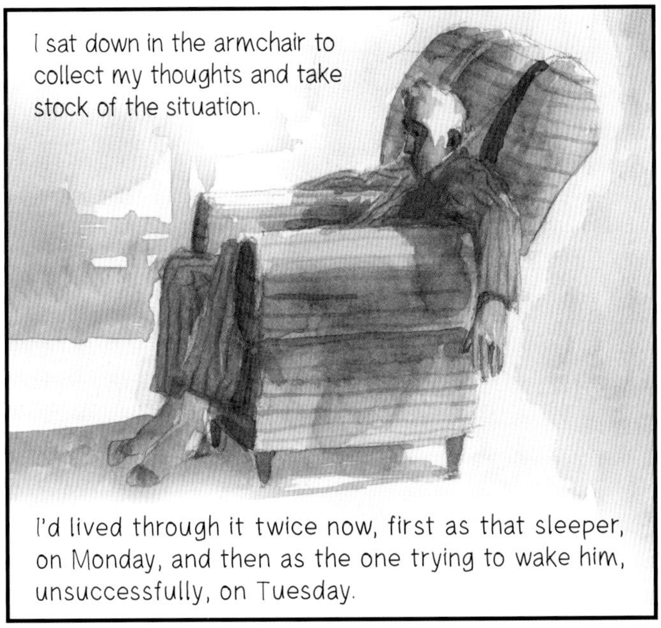
I sat down in the armchair to collect my thoughts and take stock of the situation.
I'd lived through it twice now, first as that sleeper, on Monday, and then as the one trying to wake him, unsuccessfully, on Tuesday.

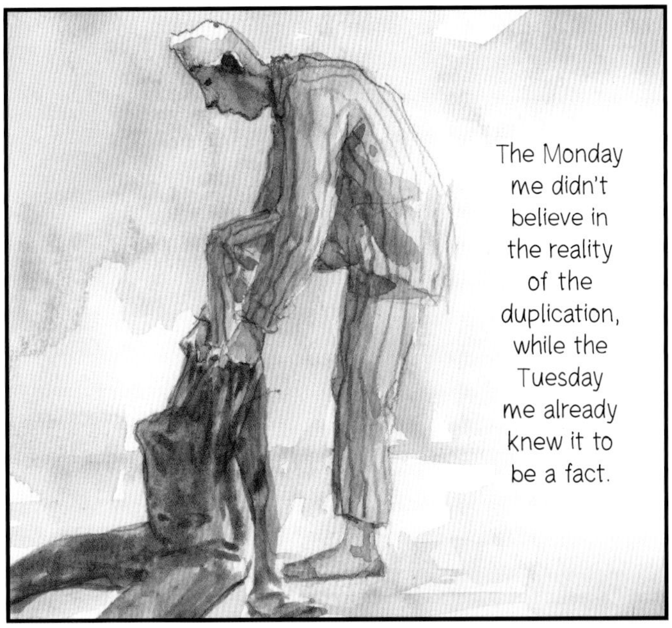
The Monday me didn't believe in the reality of the duplication, while the Tuesday me already knew it to be a fact.

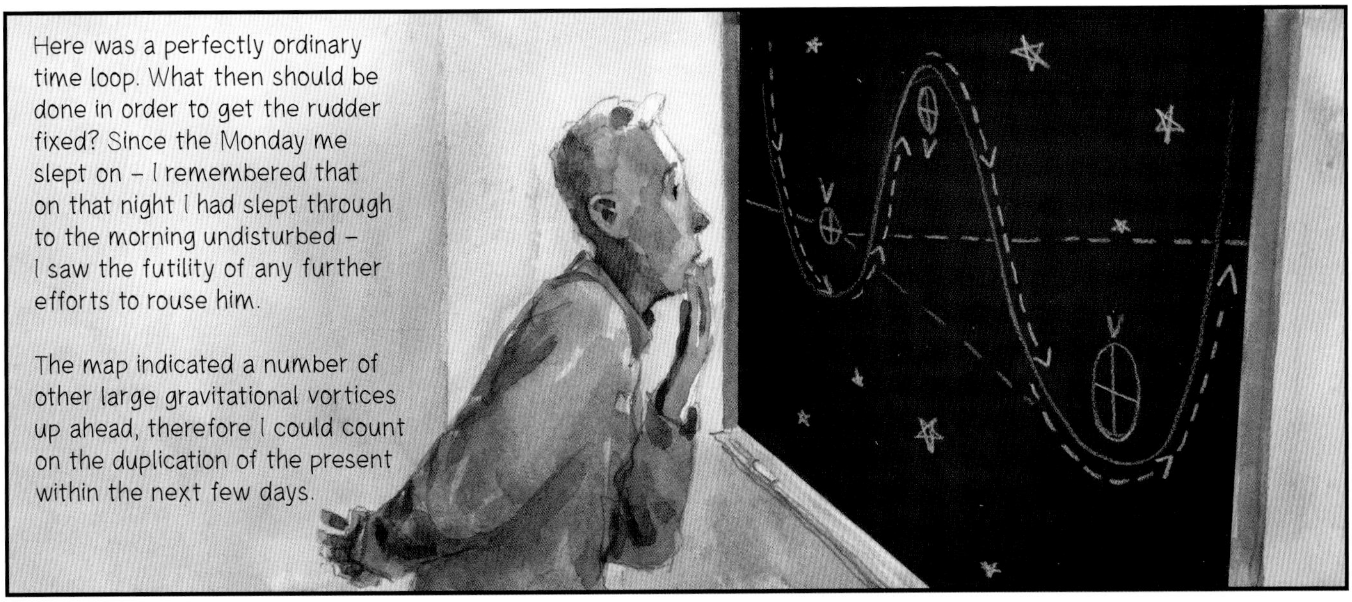
Here was a perfectly ordinary time loop. What then should be done in order to get the rudder fixed? Since the Monday me slept on – I remembered that on that night I had slept through to the morning undisturbed – I saw the futility of any further efforts to rouse him.
The map indicated a number of other large gravitational vortices up ahead, therefore I could count on the duplication of the present within the next few days.

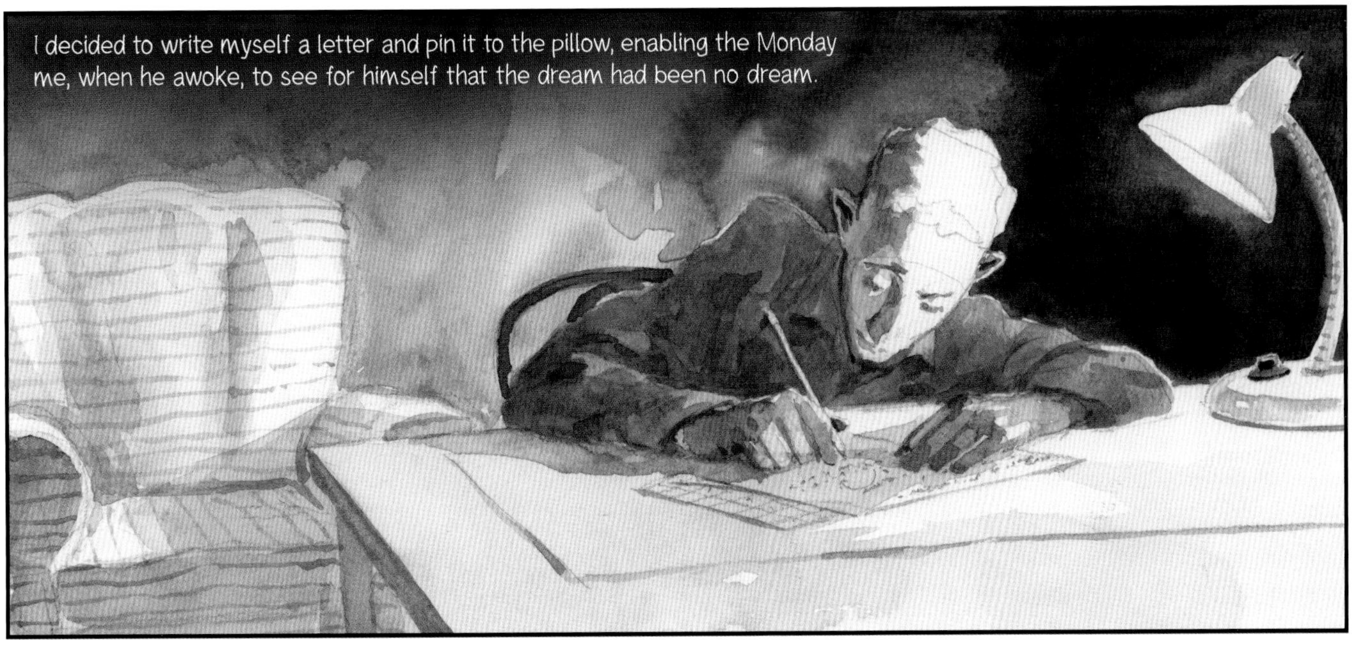
I decided to write myself a letter and pin it to the pillow, enabling the Monday me, when he awoke, to see for himself that the dream had been no dream.

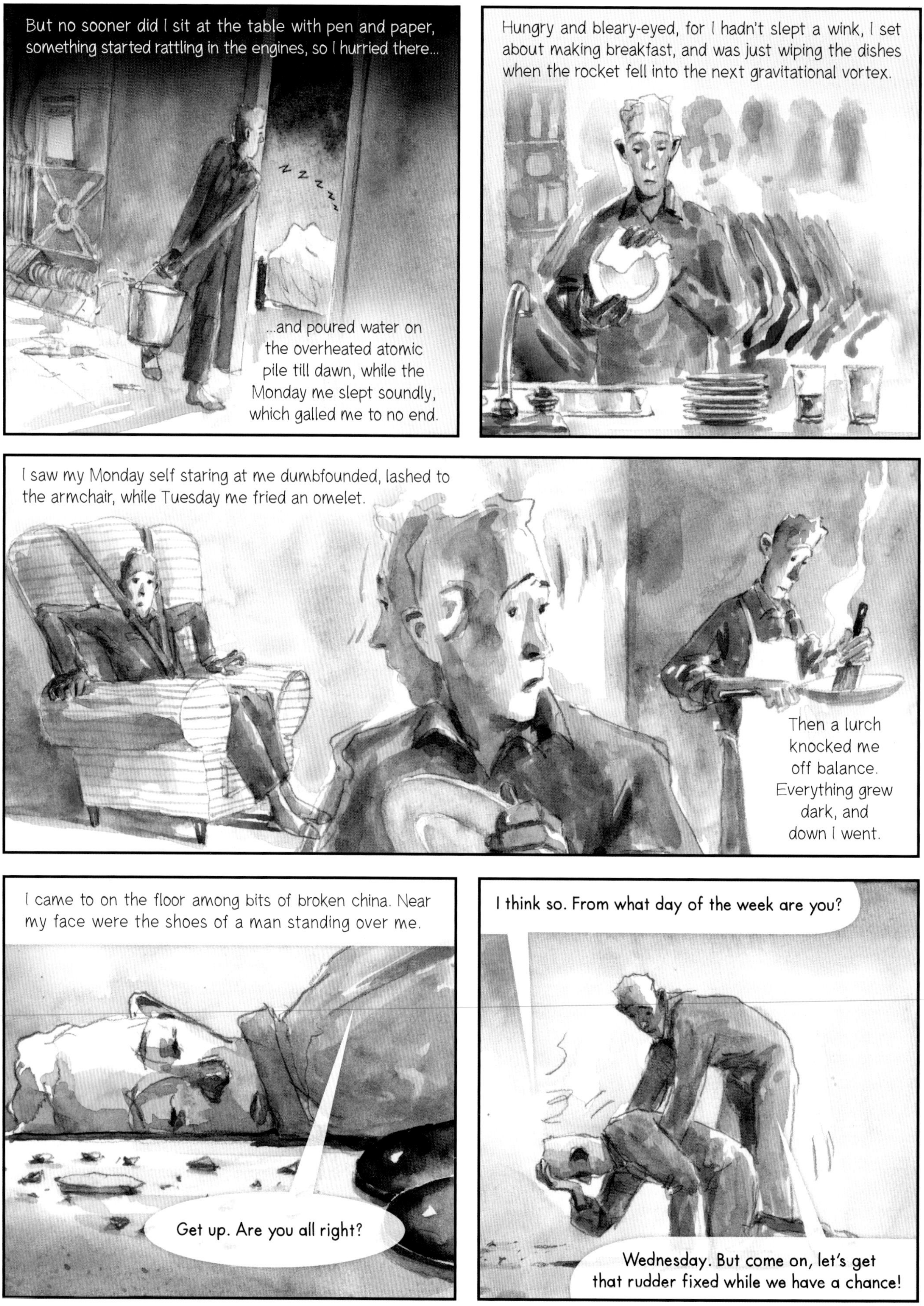
But no sooner did I sit at the table with pen and paper, something started rattling in the engines, so I hurried there...
Z Z Z Z
...and poured water on the overheated atomic pile till dawn, while the Monday me slept soundly, which galled me to no end.
Hungry and bleary-eyed, for I hadn't slept a wink, I set about making breakfast, and was just wiping the dishes when the rocket fell into the next gravitational vortex.
I saw my Monday self staring at me dumbfounded, lashed to the armchair, while Tuesday me fried an omelet.
Then a lurch knocked me off balance. Everything grew dark, and down I went.
I came to on the floor among bits of broken china. Near my face were the shoes of a man standing over me.
Get up. Are you all right?
I think so. From what day of the week are you?
Wednesday. But come on, let's get that rudder fixed while we have a chance!

Look, I'm Wednesday me and you're the Tuesday me. And as for the rocket, well, my guess is that its existence is patched, which means that in places it's a Tuesday, and in places Wednesday...

...and here and there perhaps there's even a bit of Thursday.

Time has simply become shuffled up passing through these vortices, but why should that concern us, when together we are two and therefore have a chance to fix the rudder?

No, you're wrong! If on Wednesday, where you already are, having lived through all of Tuesday, so that now Tuesday is behind you, if on Wednesday – I repeat – the rudder isn't fixed...

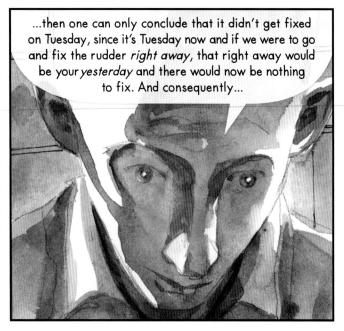

...then one can only conclude that it didn't get fixed on Tuesday, since it's Tuesday now and if we were to go and fix the rudder *right away*, that right away would be your *yesterday* and there would now be nothing to fix. And consequently...

And consequently you're as stubborn as a mule! You'll regret this! And my only consolation is that you, too, will be infuriated by your pigheadedness, just as I am now – when you yourself reach Wednesday!

Ah, wait, do you mean that on Wednesday, I being you...

...will try to convince the Tuesday me, just as you are doing here, except that everything will be reversed...

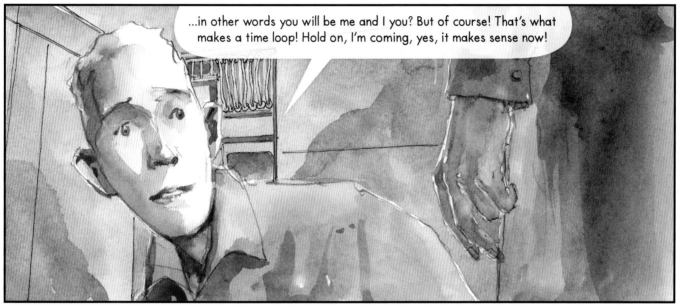

...in other words you will be me and I you? But of course! That's what makes a time loop! Hold on, I'm coming, yes, it makes sense now!

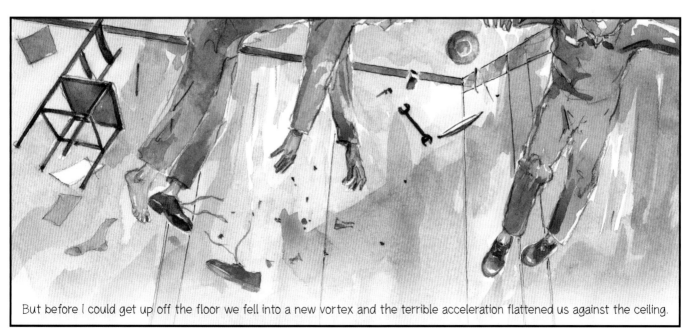

But before I could get up off the floor we fell into a new vortex and the terrible acceleration flattened us against the ceiling.

The dreadful pitching and heaving didn't let up once throughout that night from Tuesday to Wednesday.

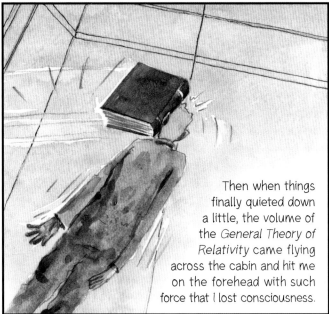

Then when things finally quieted down a little, the volume of the *General Theory of Relativity* came flying across the cabin and hit me on the forehead with such force that I lost consciousness.

When I opened my eyes I saw broken dishes and a man sprawled among them. I immediately jumped to my feet and lifted him.

Get up! Are you all right?

I think so. From what day of the week are you?

Wednesday. Come on, let's get that rudder fixed while we have the chance.

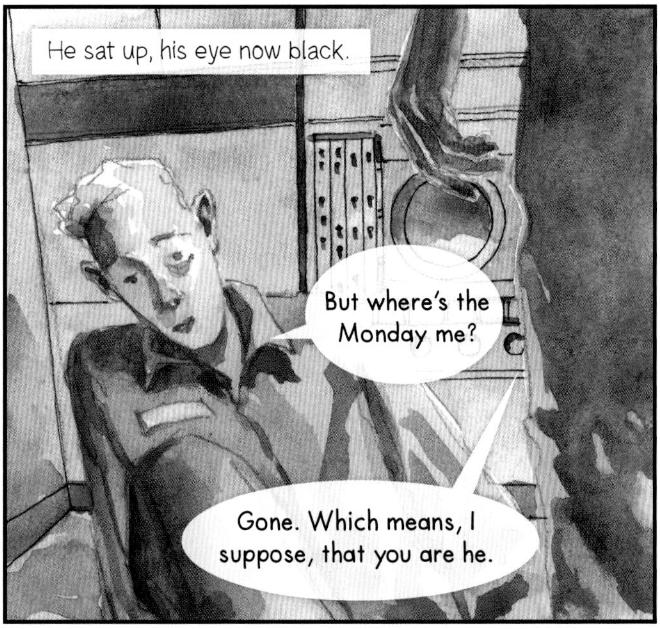
He sat up, his eye now black.
But where's the Monday me?
Gone. Which means, I suppose, that you are he.

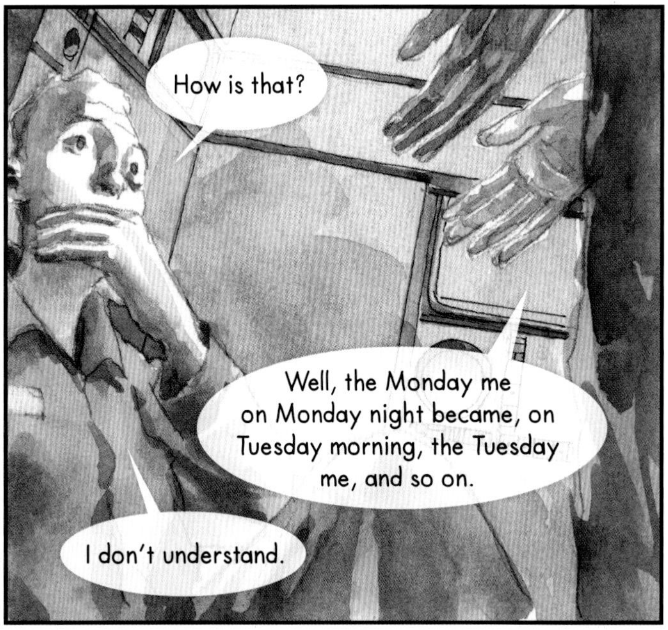
How is that?
Well, the Monday me on Monday night became, on Tuesday morning, the Tuesday me, and so on.
I don't understand.

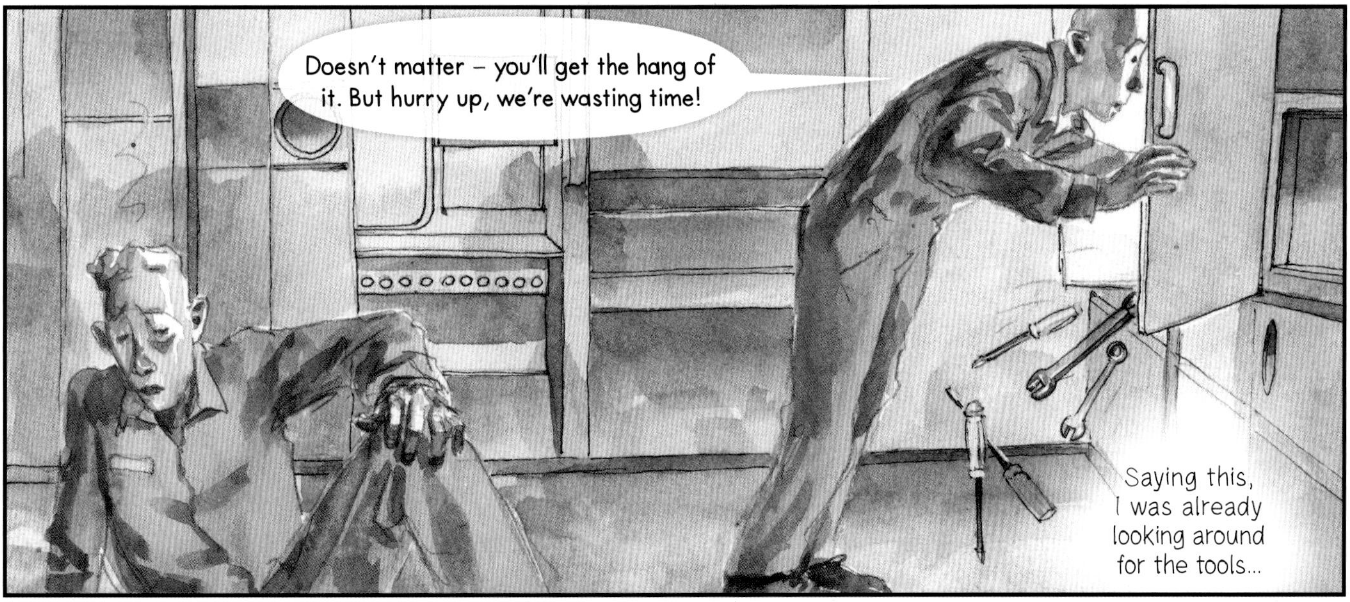
Doesn't matter – you'll get the hang of it. But hurry up, we're wasting time!
Saying this, I was already looking around for the tools...

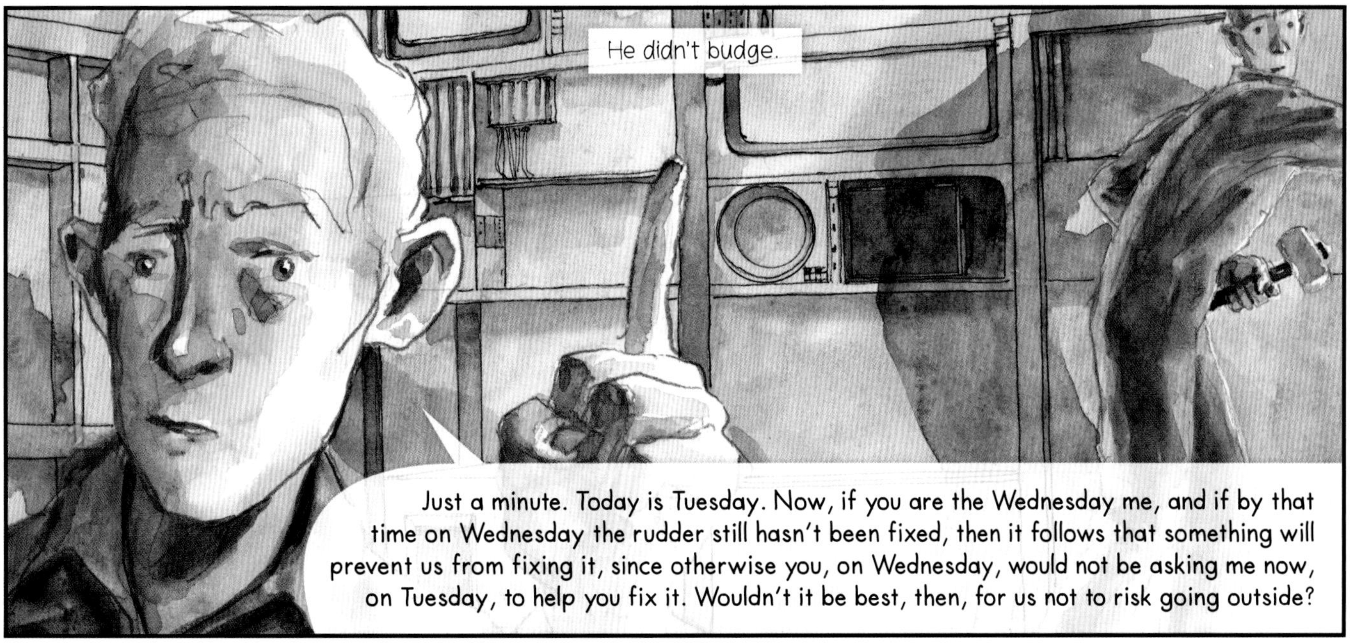
He didn't budge.
Just a minute. Today is Tuesday. Now, if you are the Wednesday me, and if by that time on Wednesday the rudder still hasn't been fixed, then it follows that something will prevent us from fixing it, since otherwise you, on Wednesday, would not be asking me now, on Tuesday, to help you fix it. Wouldn't it be best, then, for us not to risk going outside?

NONSENSE! Look, I'm the Wednesday me, you're the Tuesday me...

And so we quarreled, in opposite roles, during which he did in fact drive me into a positive fury, for he persistently refused to help me fix the rudder, and it did no good calling him pigheaded and a stubborn mule.

And when at last I managed to convince him, we were plunged into the next gravitational vortex.

I was in a cold sweat, for the thought occurred to me that we might go around and around in this time loop, repeating ourselves for eternity, but luckily that didn't happen.

By the time acceleration had slackened enough for me to stand, I was alone once more in the cabin.

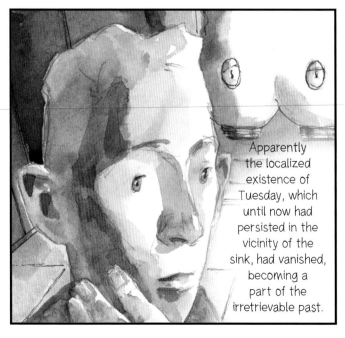

Apparently the localized existence of Tuesday, which until now had persisted in the vicinity of the sink, had vanished, becoming a part of the irretrievable past.

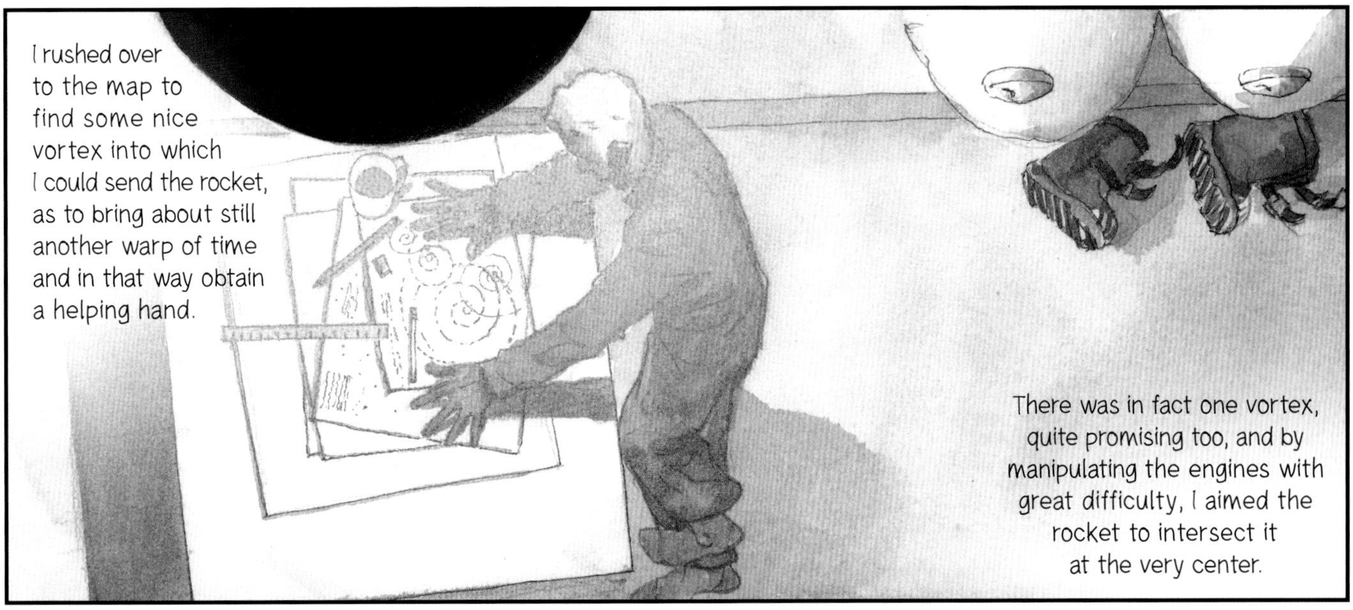
I rushed over to the map to find some nice vortex into which I could send the rocket, as to bring about still another warp of time and in that way obtain a helping hand.
There was in fact one vortex, quite promising too, and by manipulating the engines with great difficulty, I aimed the rocket to intersect it at the very center.

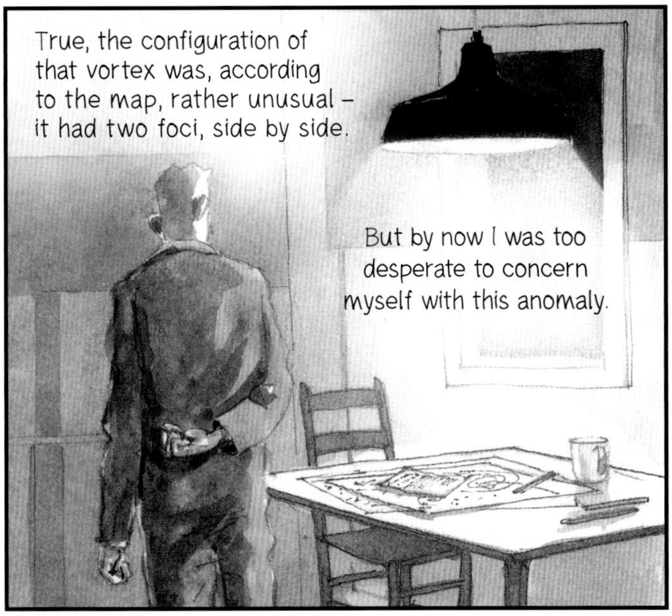
True, the configuration of that vortex was, according to the map, rather unusual – it had two foci, side by side.
But by now I was too desperate to concern myself with this anomaly.

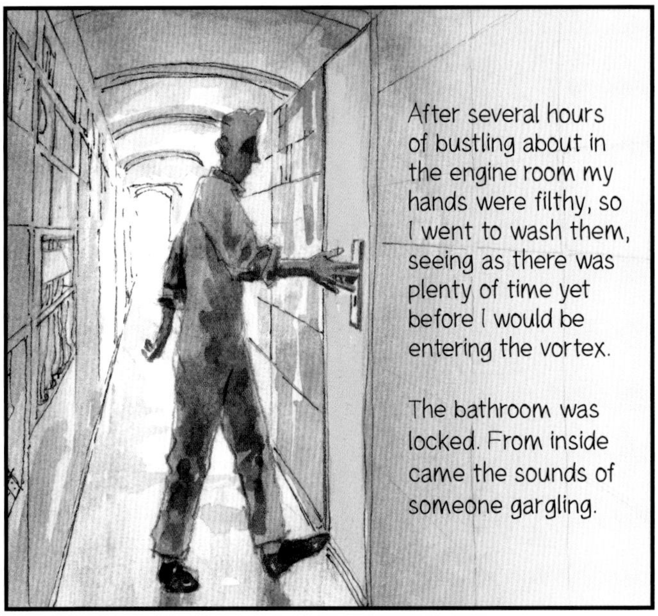
After several hours of bustling about in the engine room my hands were filthy, so I went to wash them, seeing as there was plenty of time yet before I would be entering the vortex.
The bathroom was locked. From inside came the sounds of someone gargling.

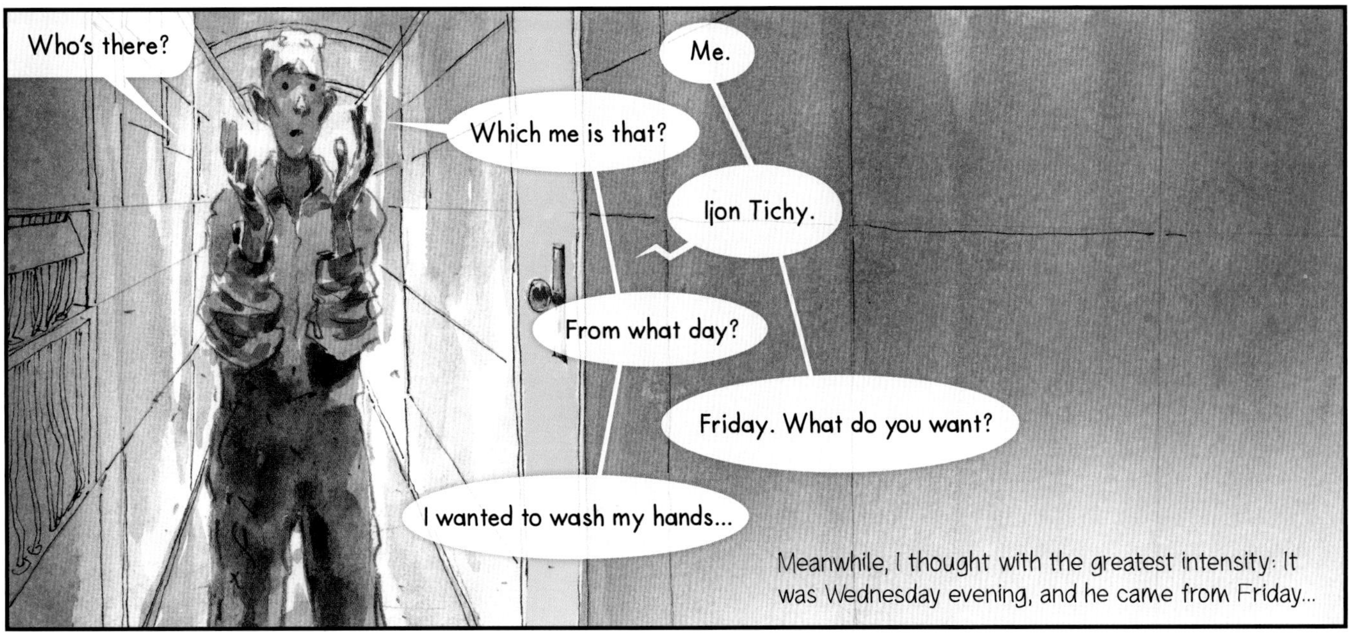
Who's there?
Me.
Which me is that?
Ijon Tichy.
From what day?
Friday. What do you want?
I wanted to wash my hands...
Meanwhile, I thought with the greatest intensity: It was Wednesday evening, and he came from Friday...

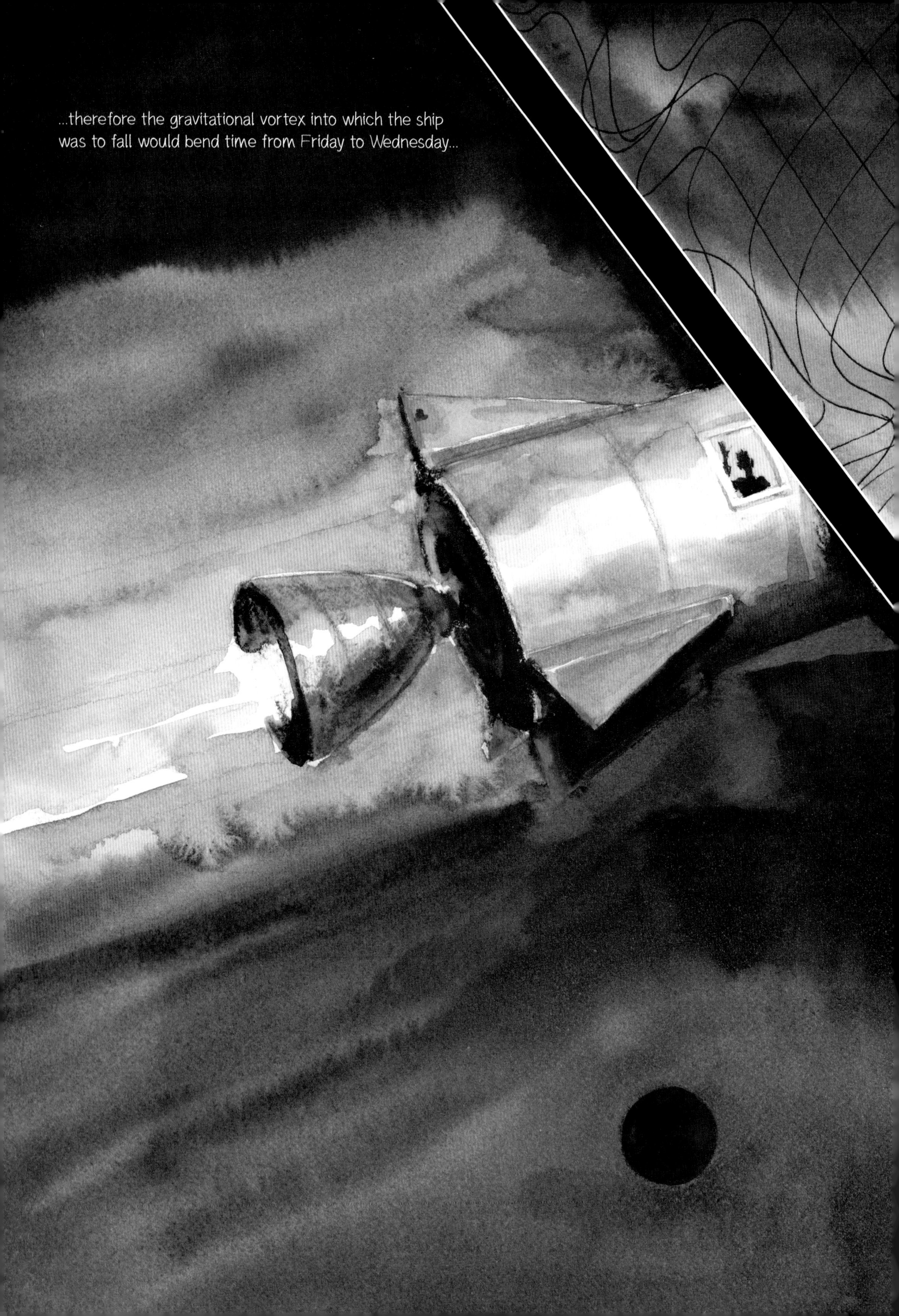
...therefore the gravitational vortex into which the ship was to fall would bend time from Friday to Wednesday...

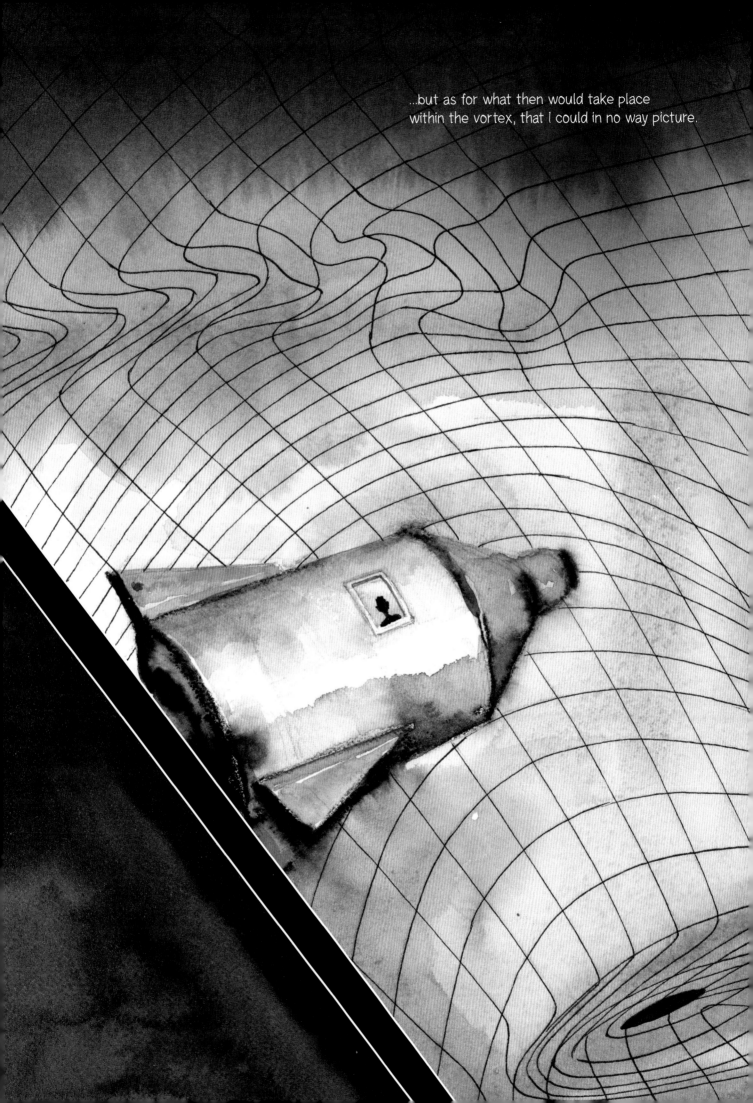

...but as for what then would take place
within the vortex, that I could in no way picture.

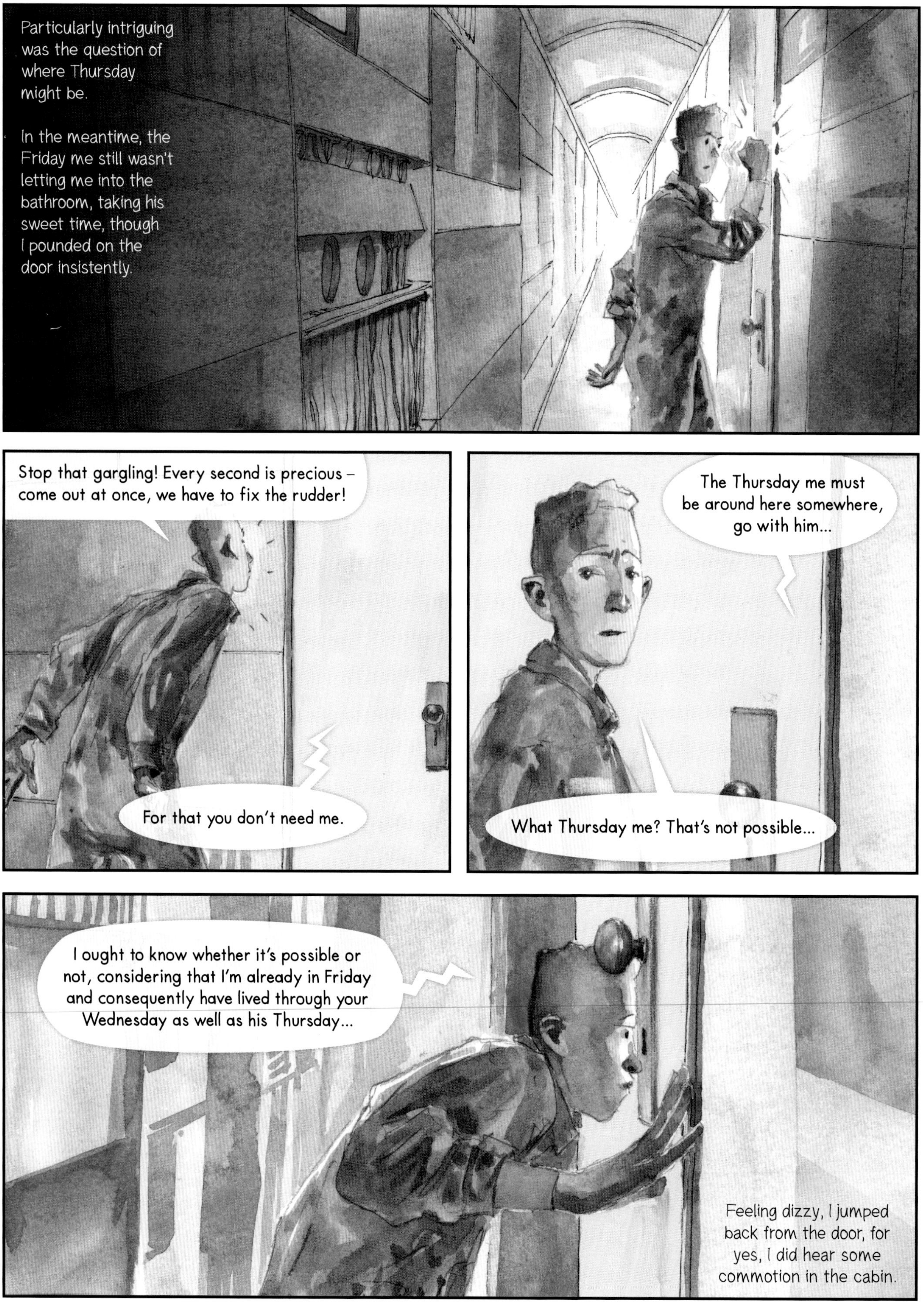
Particularly intriguing was the question of where Thursday might be.
In the meantime, the Friday me still wasn't letting me into the bathroom, taking his sweet time, though I pounded on the door insistently.
Stop that gargling! Every second is precious – come out at once, we have to fix the rudder!
For that you don't need me.
The Thursday me must be around here somewhere, go with him...
What Thursday me? That's not possible...
I ought to know whether it's possible or not, considering that I'm already in Friday and consequently have lived through your Wednesday as well as his Thursday...
Feeling dizzy, I jumped back from the door, for yes, I did hear some commotion in the cabin.

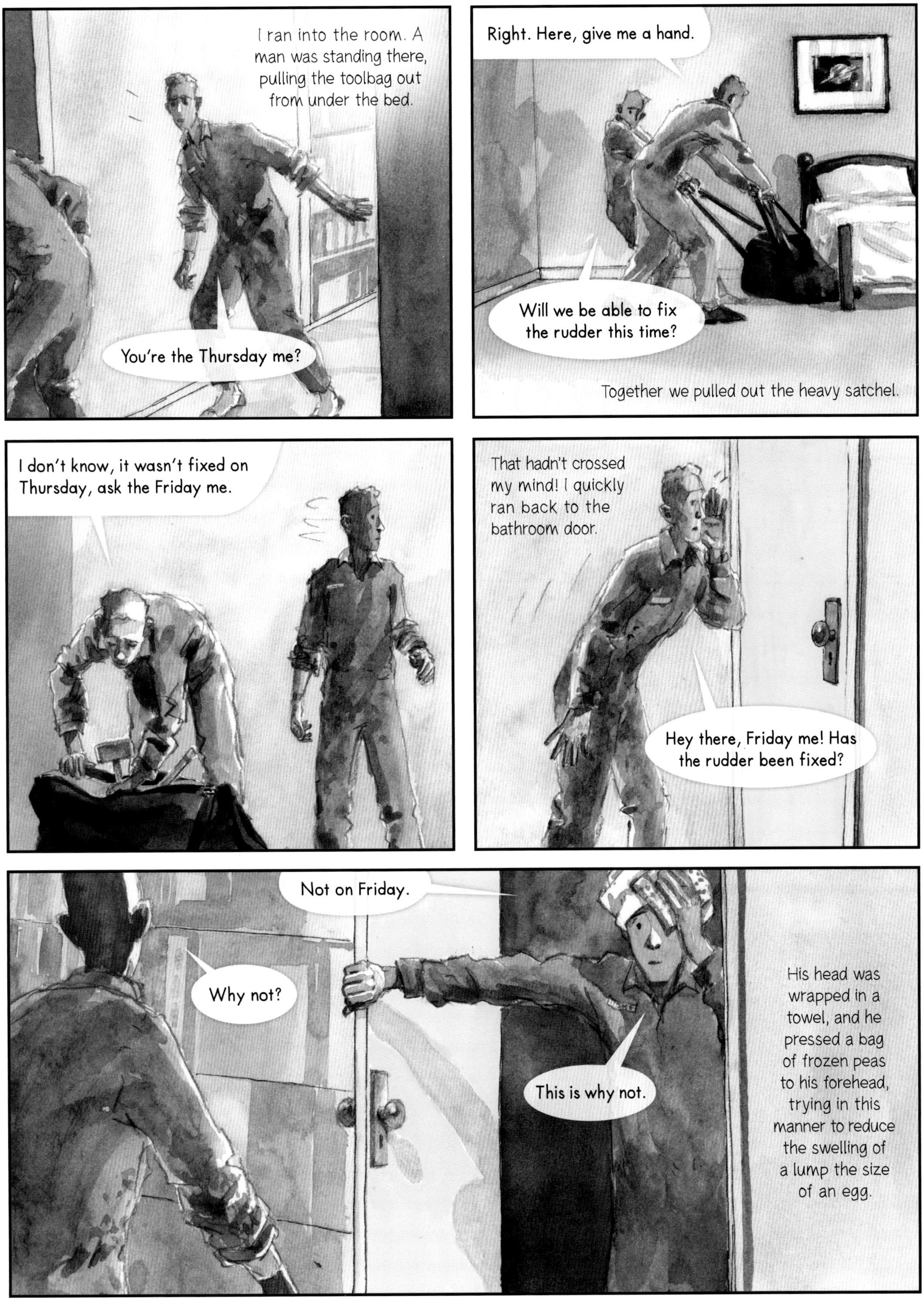

I ran into the room. A man was standing there, pulling the toolbag out from under the bed.
You're the Thursday me?
Right. Here, give me a hand.
Will we be able to fix the rudder this time?
Together we pulled out the heavy satchel.
I don't know, it wasn't fixed on Thursday, ask the Friday me.
That hadn't crossed my mind! I quickly ran back to the bathroom door.
Hey there, Friday me! Has the rudder been fixed?
Not on Friday.
Why not?
This is why not.
His head was wrapped in a towel, and he pressed a bag of frozen peas to his forehead, trying in this manner to reduce the swelling of a lump the size of an egg.

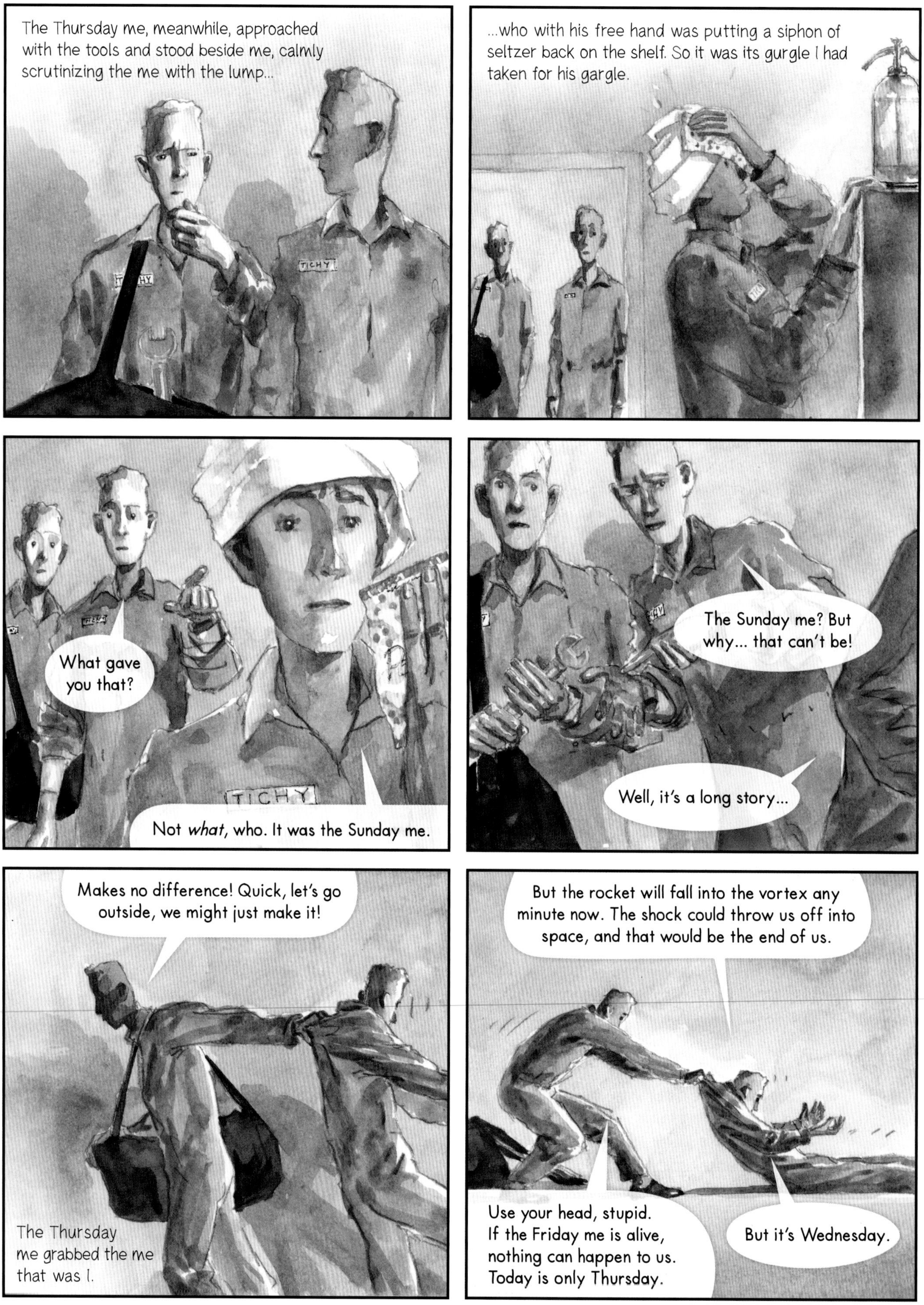
The Thursday me, meanwhile, approached with the tools and stood beside me, calmly scrutinizing the me with the lump...
TICHY
...who with his free hand was putting a siphon of seltzer back on the shelf. So it was its gurgle I had taken for his gargle.
What gave you that?
TICHY
Not *what*, who. It was the Sunday me.
The Sunday me? But why... that can't be!
Well, it's a long story...
Makes no difference! Quick, let's go outside, we might just make it!
The Thursday me grabbed the me that was I.
But the rocket will fall into the vortex any minute now. The shock could throw us off into space, and that would be the end of us.
Use your head, stupid. If the Friday me is alive, nothing can happen to us. Today is only Thursday.
But it's Wednesday.

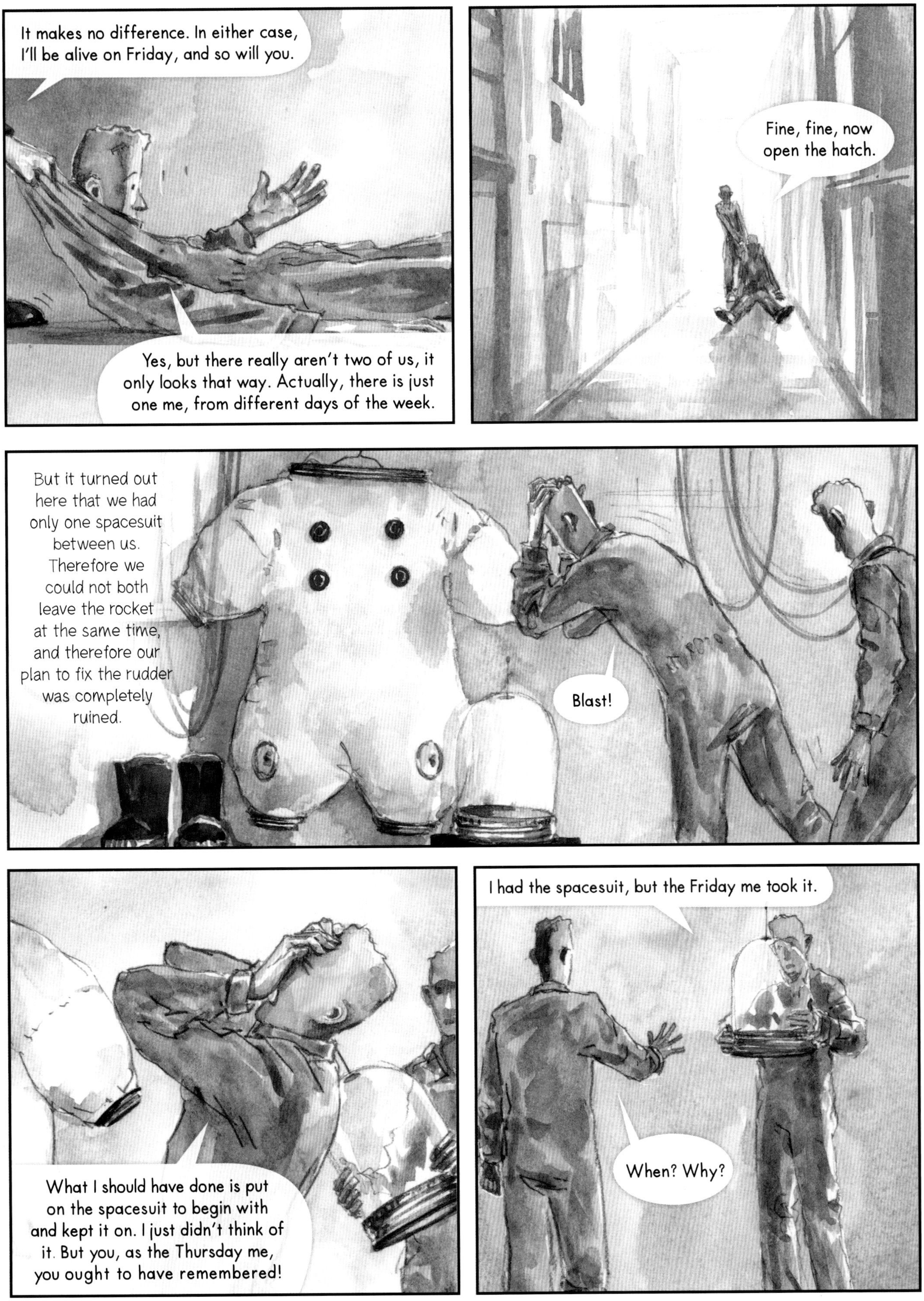
It makes no difference. In either case, I'll be alive on Friday, and so will you.
Yes, but there really aren't two of us, it only looks that way. Actually, there is just one me, from different days of the week.
Fine, fine, now open the hatch.
But it turned out here that we had only one spacesuit between us. Therefore we could not both leave the rocket at the same time, and therefore our plan to fix the rudder was completely ruined.
Blast!
What I should have done is put on the spacesuit to begin with and kept it on. I just didn't think of it. But you, as the Thursday me, you ought to have remembered!
I had the spacesuit, but the Friday me took it.
When? Why?

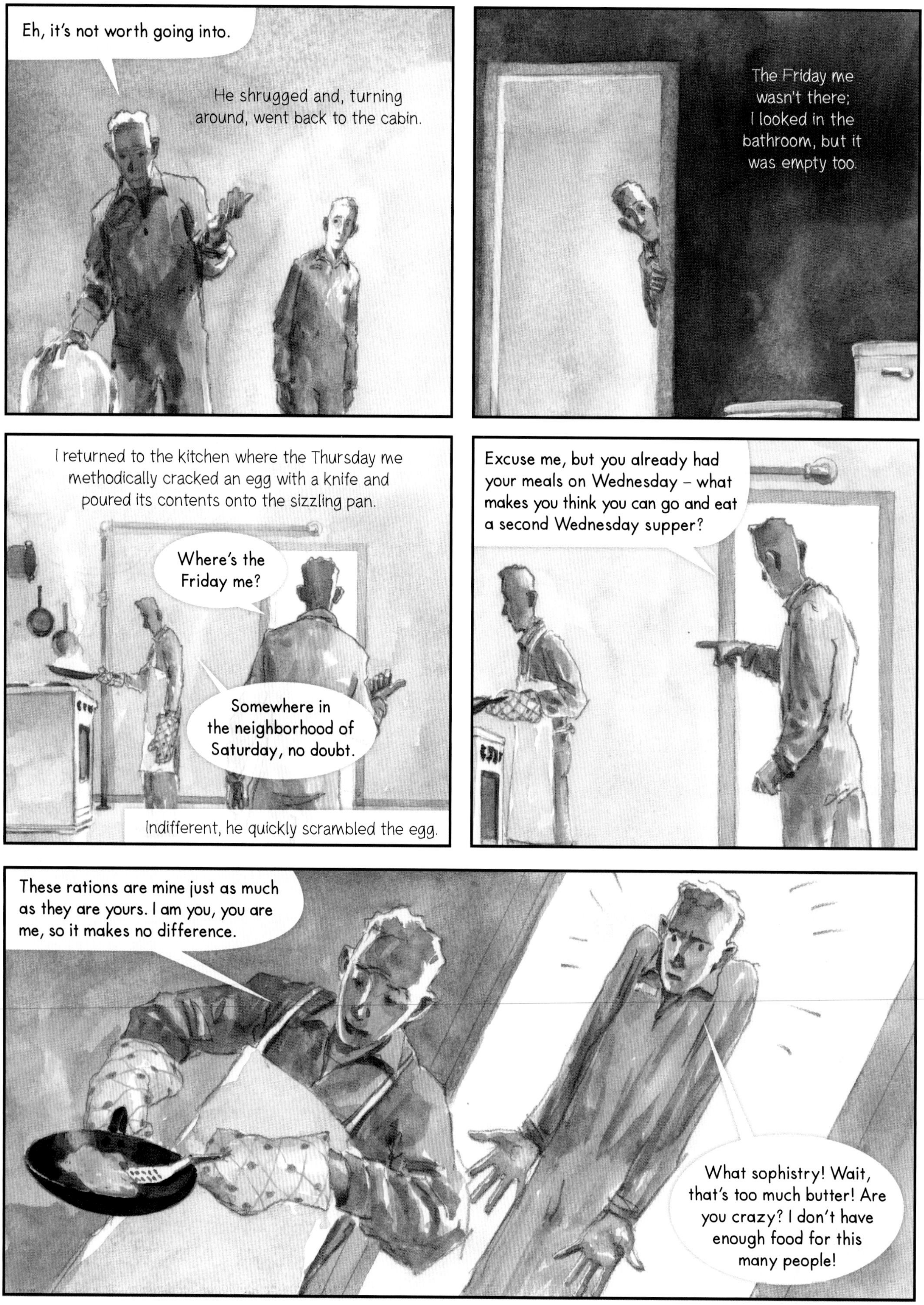
Eh, it's not worth going into.
He shrugged and, turning around, went back to the cabin.
The Friday me wasn't there; I looked in the bathroom, but it was empty too.
I returned to the kitchen where the Thursday me methodically cracked an egg with a knife and poured its contents onto the sizzling pan.
Where's the Friday me?
Somewhere in the neighborhood of Saturday, no doubt.
Indifferent, he quickly scrambled the egg.
Excuse me, but you already had your meals on Wednesday – what makes you think you can go and eat a second Wednesday supper?
These rations are mine just as much as they are yours. I am you, you are me, so it makes no difference.
What sophistry! Wait, that's too much butter! Are you crazy? I don't have enough food for this many people!

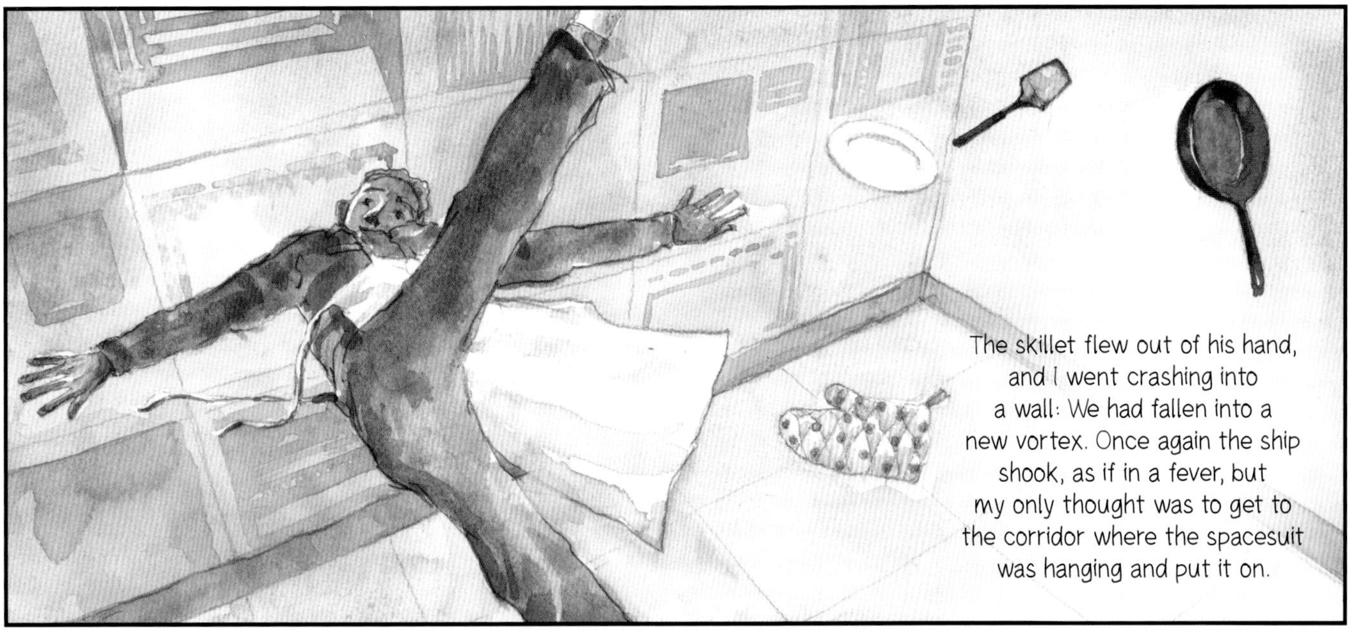
The skillet flew out of his hand, and I went crashing into a wall: We had fallen into a new vortex. Once again the ship shook, as if in a fever, but my only thought was to get to the corridor where the spacesuit was hanging and put it on.

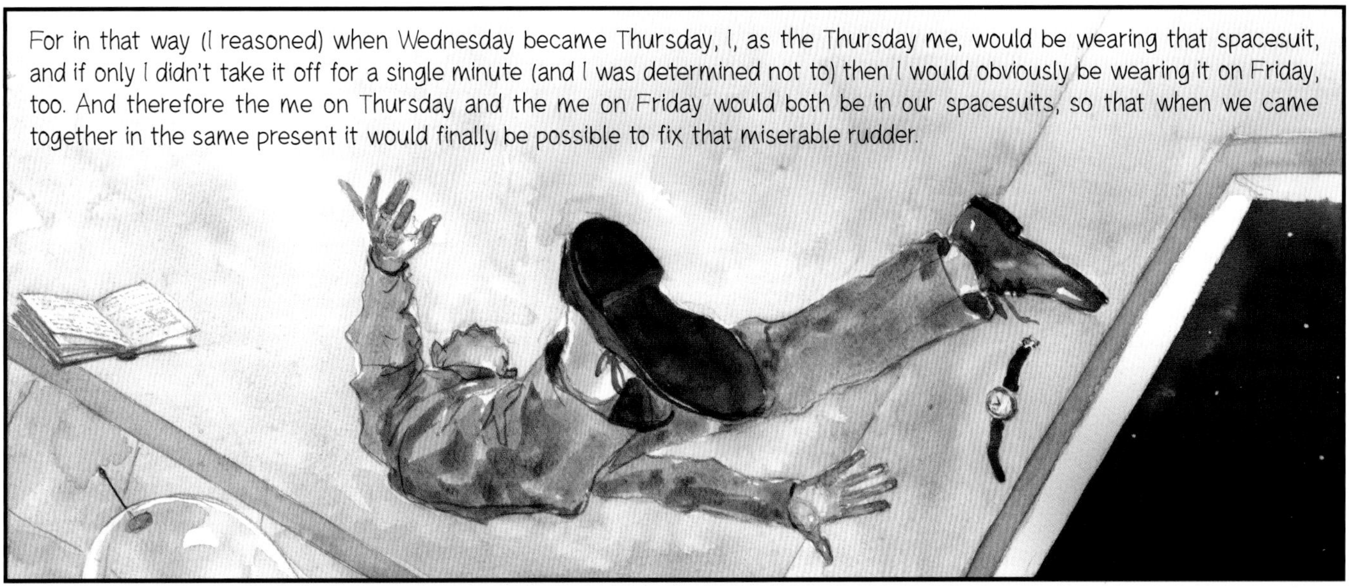
For in that way (I reasoned) when Wednesday became Thursday, I, as the Thursday me, would be wearing that spacesuit, and if only I didn't take it off for a single minute (and I was determined not to) then I would obviously be wearing it on Friday, too. And therefore the me on Thursday and the me on Friday would both be in our spacesuits, so that when we came together in the same present it would finally be possible to fix that miserable rudder.

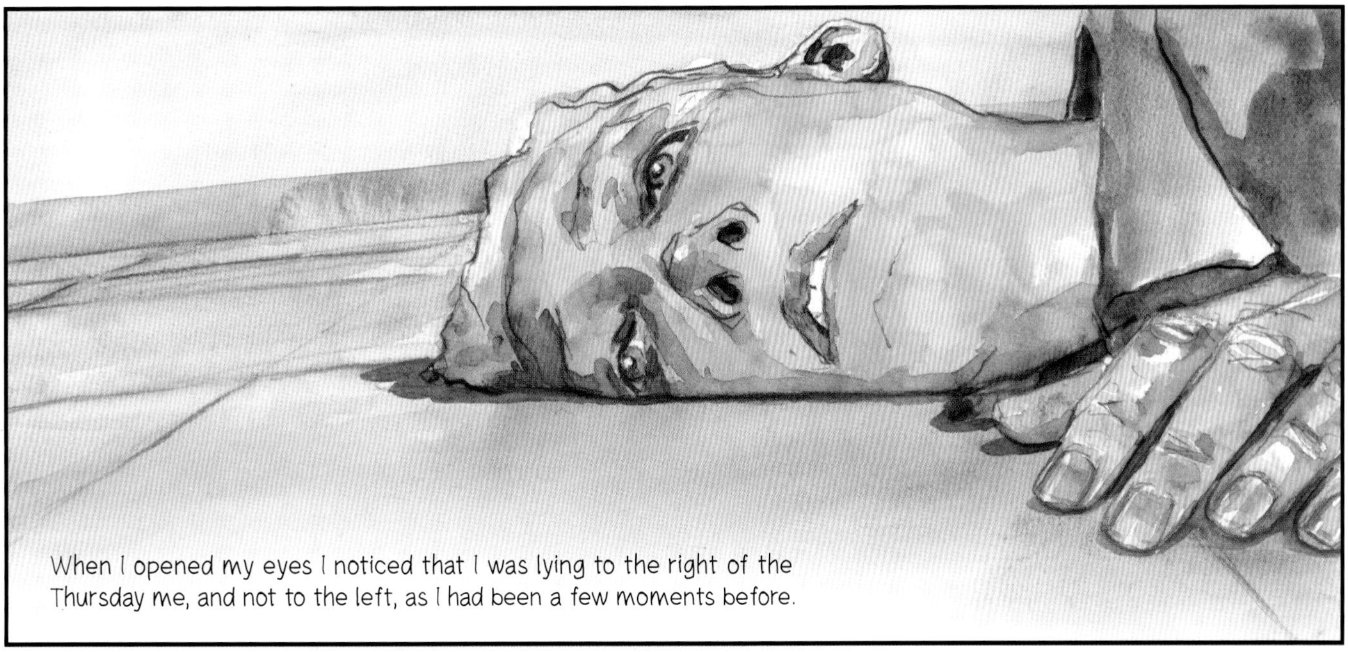
When I opened my eyes I noticed that I was lying to the right of the Thursday me, and not to the left, as I had been a few moments before.

Now while it had been easy enough for me to develop this plan about the spacesuit, it was considerably more difficult to put it into action, since with the growing gravitation I could hardly move.

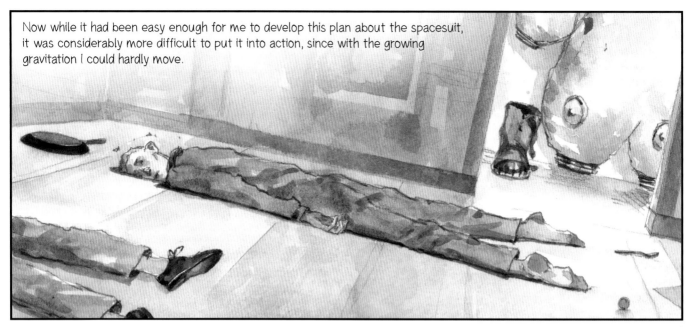

When it weakened just a little, I began to inch my way across the floor – in the direction of the door that led to the corridor.

Meanwhile, I noticed that the Thursday me was likewise heading for the door, crawling on his belly toward the corridor. At last, after about an hour, when the vortex had reached its widest point, we met at the threshold...

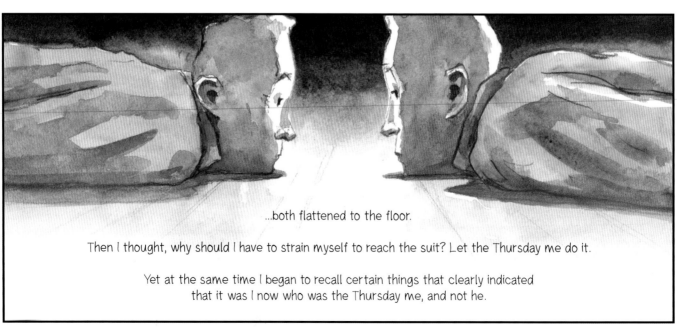

...both flattened to the floor.

Then I thought, why should I have to strain myself to reach the suit? Let the Thursday me do it.

Yet at the same time I began to recall certain things that clearly indicated that it was I now who was the Thursday me, and not he.

I looked him in the eye.

What day of the week are you?

He groaned.

Thursday me.

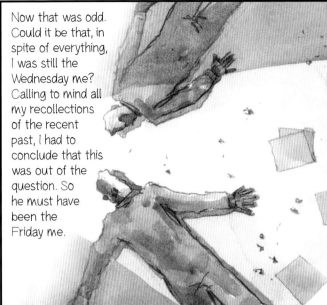

Now that was odd. Could it be that, in spite of everything, I was still the Wednesday me? Calling to mind all my recollections of the recent past, I had to conclude that this was out of the question. So he must have been the Friday me.

For if he had preceded me by a day before, then he was surely a day ahead now. I waited for him to head for the suit, but apparently he expected the same of me.

The gravitation had now subsided noticeably, so I got up and ran to the corridor. Just as I grabbed the spacesuit, he tripped me, pulling it out of my hands, and I fell flat on my face.

You plog! Tripping your own self – that's really low!

He ignored me, stepping calmly into the spacesuit.

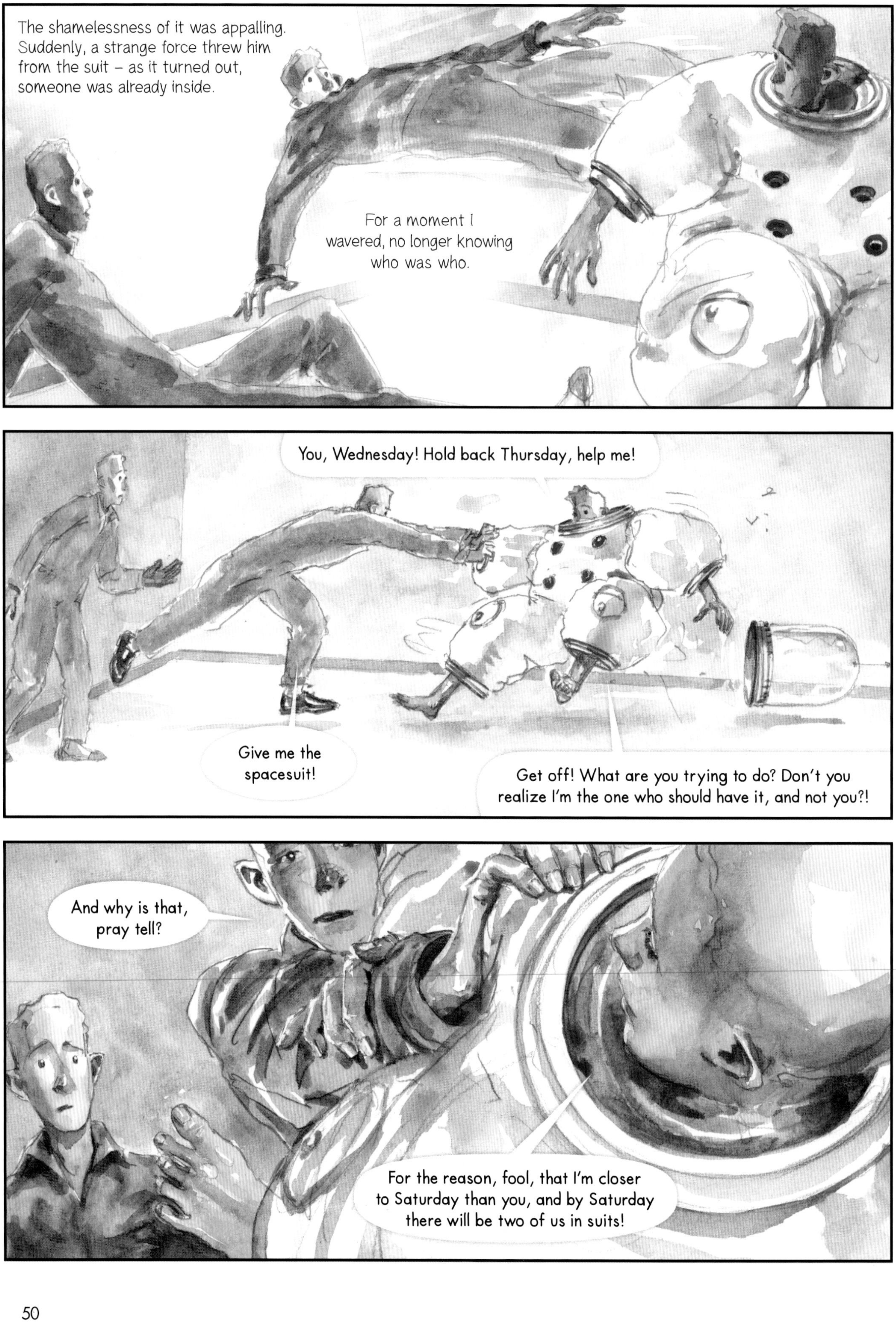
The shamelessness of it was appalling. Suddenly, a strange force threw him from the suit – as it turned out, someone was already inside.
For a moment I wavered, no longer knowing who was who.
You, Wednesday! Hold back Thursday, help me!
Give me the spacesuit!
Get off! What are you trying to do? Don't you realize I'm the one who should have it, and not you?!
And why is that, pray tell?
For the reason, fool, that I'm closer to Saturday than you, and by Saturday there will be two of us in suits!

I entered into their argument.

But that's ridiculous. At best you'll be alone in the suit on Saturday, like an absolute idiot, and won't be able to do a thing.

Let me have the suit: If I put it on now, then you'll be wearing it on Friday as the Friday me, and I will wear it on Saturday as the Saturday me, and so you see there will then be two of us, and with two suits.

Come on, Thursday, give me a hand!

Wait!

I had forcibly yanked the spacesuit off the Friday me.

In the first place, there is no one here for you to call Thursday, since midnight has passed and *you* are now the Thursday me...

...and in the second place, it'll be better if I stay in the spacesuit. The spacesuit won't do you a bit of good.

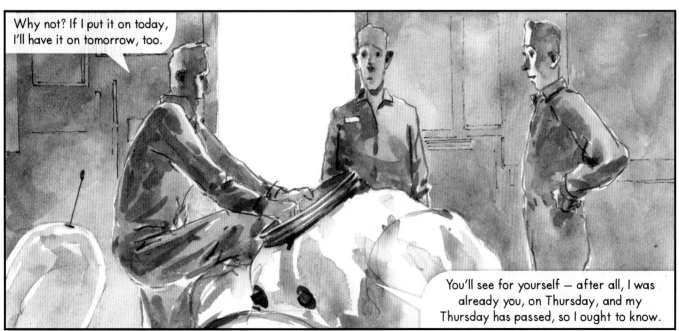

Why not? If I put it on today, I'll have it on tomorrow, too.

You'll see for yourself — after all, I was already you, on Thursday, and my Thursday has passed, so I ought to know.

51

Enough talk. Let go of it this instant!

But he grabbed it from me and I chased him, first through the engine room and then into the cabin. It somehow worked out that there were only two of us now.

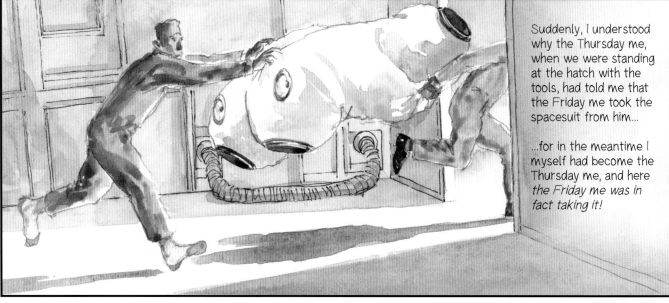

Suddenly, I understood why the Thursday me, when we were standing at the hatch with the tools, had told me that the Friday me took the spacesuit from him...

...for in the meantime I myself had become the Thursday me, and here *the Friday me was in fact taking it!*

Just you wait. I'll take care of you!

But I had no intention of giving in that easily.

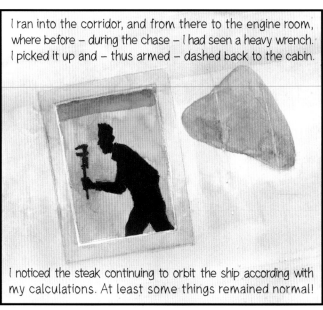

I ran into the corridor, and from there to the engine room, where before – during the chase – I had seen a heavy wrench. I picked it up and – thus armed – dashed back to the cabin.

I noticed the steak continuing to orbit the ship according with my calculations. At least some things remained normal!

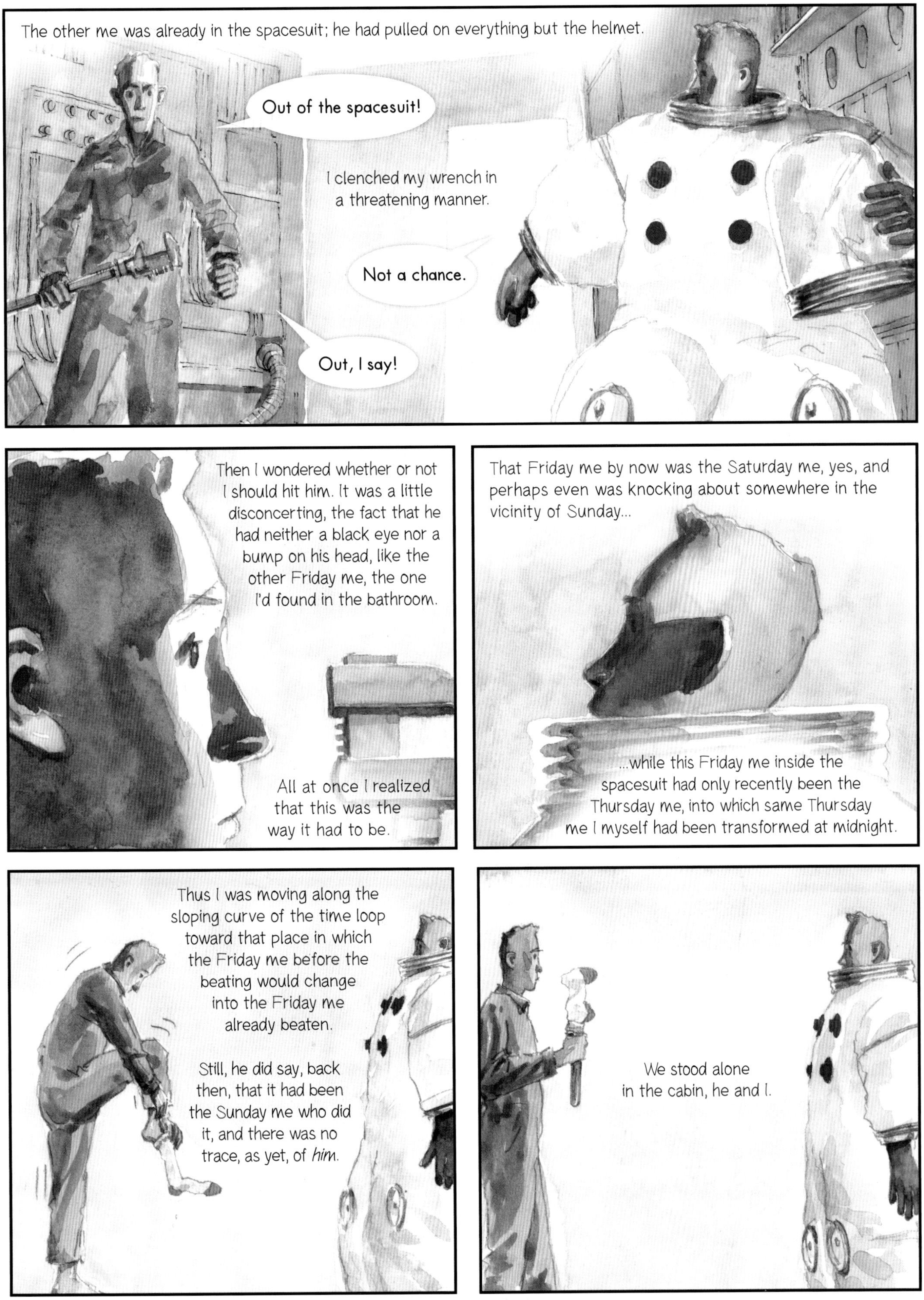
The other me was already in the spacesuit; he had pulled on everything but the helmet.
Out of the spacesuit!
I clenched my wrench in a threatening manner.
Not a chance.
Out, I say!
Then I wondered whether or not I should hit him. It was a little disconcerting, the fact that he had neither a black eye nor a bump on his head, like the other Friday me, the one I'd found in the bathroom.
All at once I realized that this was the way it had to be.
That Friday me by now was the Saturday me, yes, and perhaps even was knocking about somewhere in the vicinity of Sunday...
...while this Friday me inside the spacesuit had only recently been the Thursday me, into which same Thursday me I myself had been transformed at midnight.
Thus I was moving along the sloping curve of the time loop toward that place in which the Friday me before the beating would change into the Friday me already beaten.
Still, he did say, back then, that it had been the Sunday me who did it, and there was no trace, as yet, of *him*.
We stood alone in the cabin, he and I.

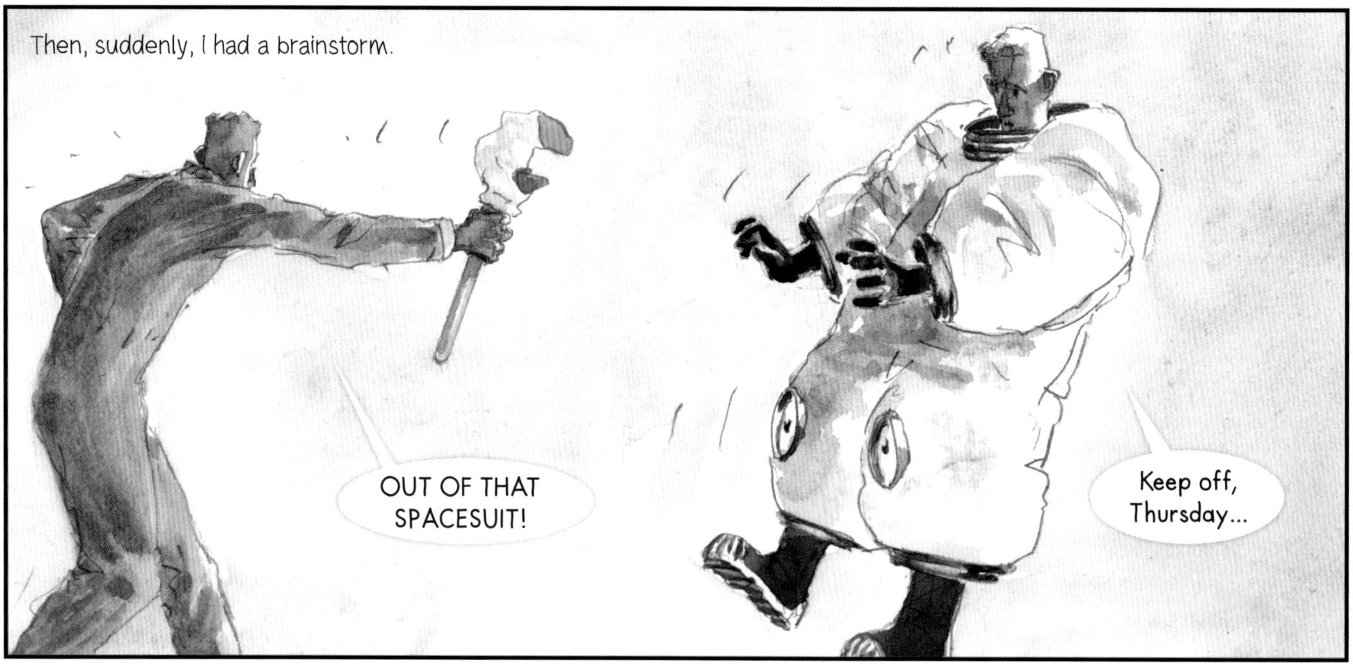
Then, suddenly, I had a brainstorm.
OUT OF THAT SPACESUIT!
Keep off, Thursday...

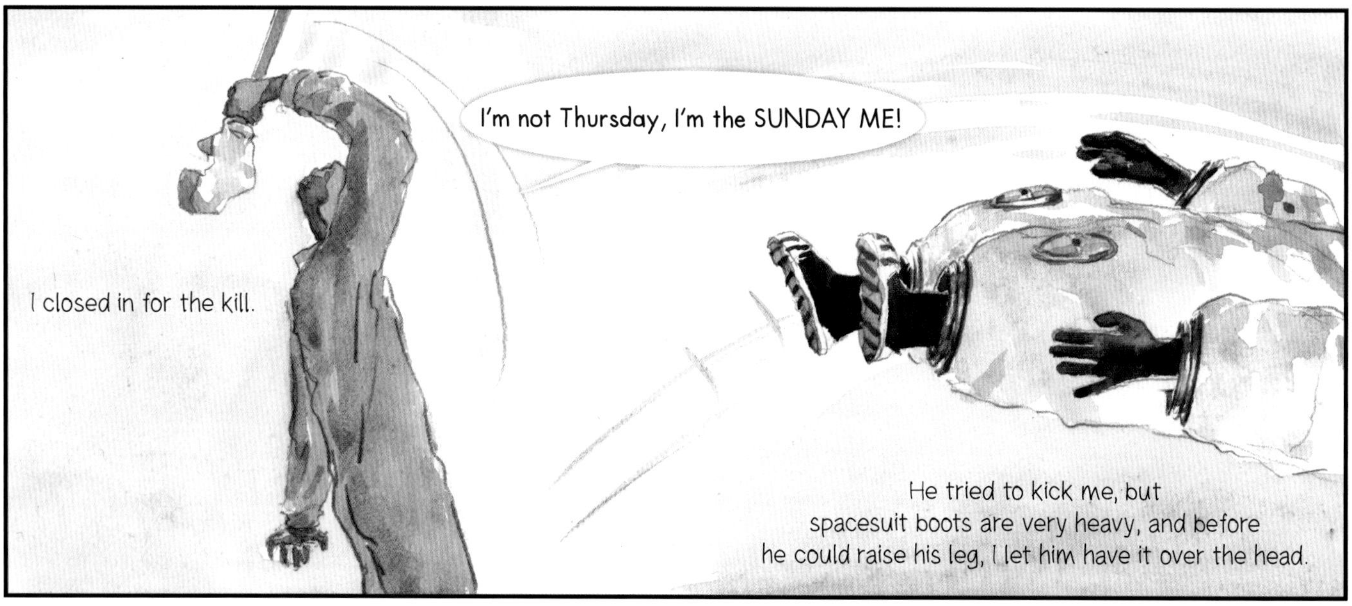
I'm not Thursday, I'm the SUNDAY ME!
I closed in for the kill.
He tried to kick me, but spacesuit boots are very heavy, and before he could raise his leg, I let him have it over the head.

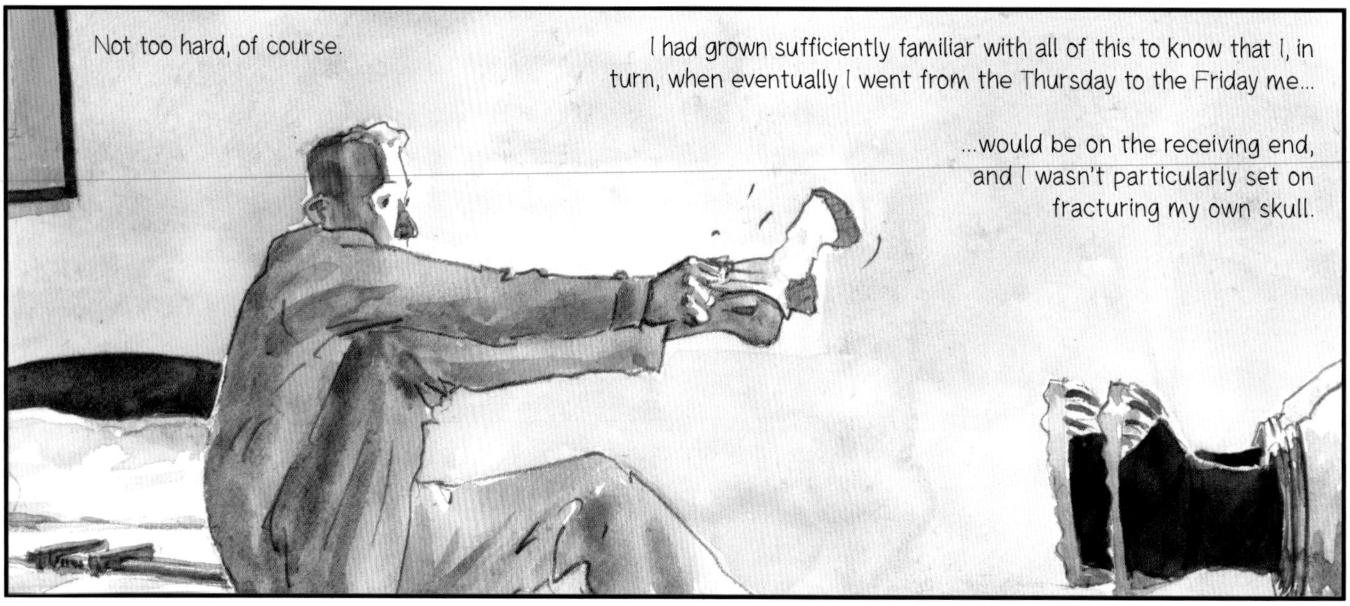
Not too hard, of course.
I had grown sufficiently familiar with all of this to know that I, in turn, when eventually I went from the Thursday to the Friday me...
...would be on the receiving end, and I wasn't particularly set on fracturing my own skull.

The Friday me groaned, holding his head, and I snatched the spacesuit off him.

He made for the bathroom on wobbly legs, muttering,

Where's the cotton... where's the seltzer... ice pack...

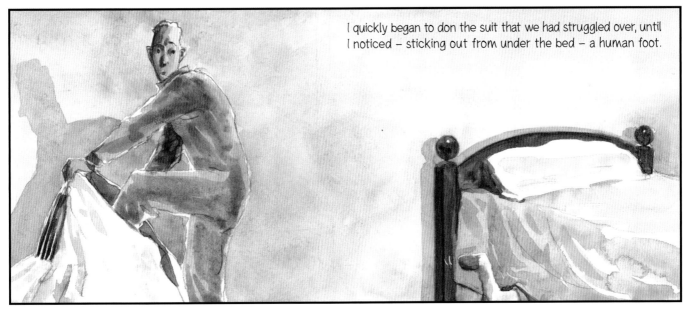

I quickly began to don the suit that we had struggled over, until I noticed – sticking out from under the bed – a human foot.

I took a closer look....

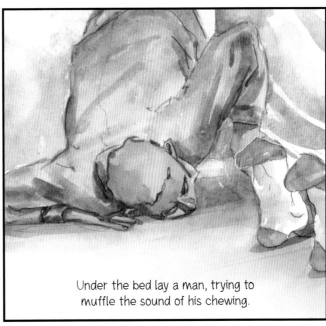

Under the bed lay a man, trying to muffle the sound of his chewing.

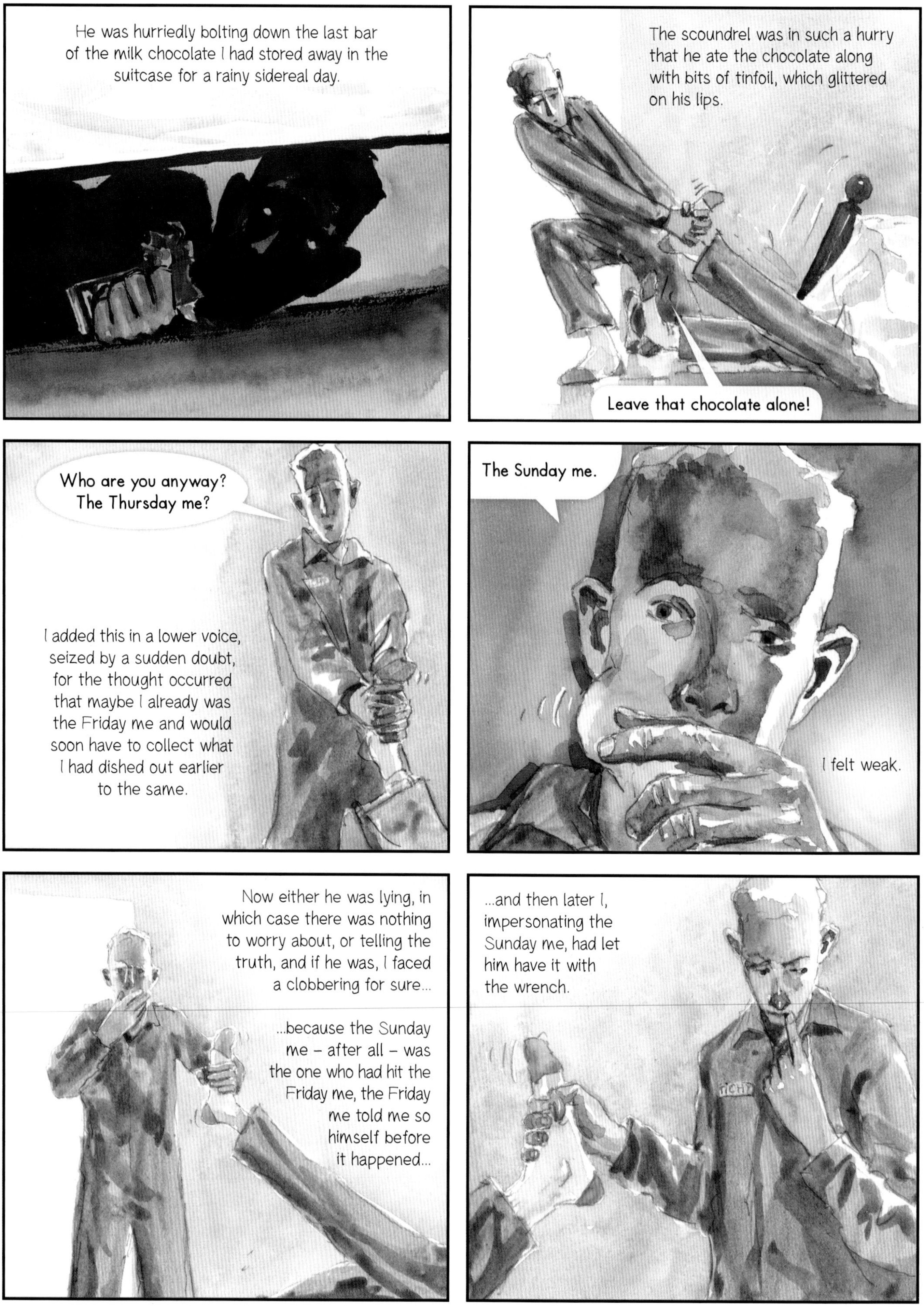
He was hurriedly bolting down the last bar of the milk chocolate I had stored away in the suitcase for a rainy sidereal day.
The scoundrel was in such a hurry that he ate the chocolate along with bits of tinfoil, which glittered on his lips.
Leave that chocolate alone!
Who are you anyway? The Thursday me?
I added this in a lower voice, seized by a sudden doubt, for the thought occurred that maybe I already was the Friday me and would soon have to collect what I had dished out earlier to the same.
The Sunday me.
I felt weak.
Now either he was lying, in which case there was nothing to worry about, or telling the truth, and if he was, I faced a clobbering for sure...
...because the Sunday me – after all – was the one who had hit the Friday me, the Friday me told me so himself before it happened...
...and then later I, impersonating the Sunday me, had let him have it with the wrench.

But on the other hand, I said to myself, even if he's lying and not the Sunday me, it's still quite possible that he's a later me than me...

...and if he is a later me, he remembers everything that I do.

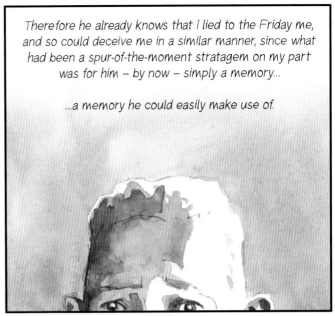

Therefore he already knows that I lied to the Friday me, and so could deceive me in a similar manner, since what had been a spur-of-the-moment stratagem on my part was for him – by now – simply a memory...

...a memory he could easily make use of.

A new thought struck me:

If you're the Sunday me, where's your spacesuit?

I'll have it in a minute...

He said this calmly, and then I noticed the pipe in his hand...

The next thing I saw was a bright flash, like a few dozen supernovas going off at once, after which I lost consciousness.

I came to on the floor of the bathroom; someone was banging on the door. I began to attend to my bruises and bumps, but he kept pounding away. It turned out to be the Wednesday me.

After a while I showed him my battered head, he went with the Thursday me for the tools, then there was a lot of running around and yanking off of spacesuits.

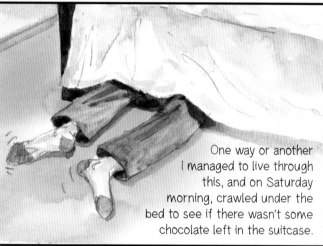

One way or another I managed to live through this, and on Saturday morning, crawled under the bed to see if there wasn't some chocolate left in the suitcase.

Someone started pulling at my foot as I ate the last bar, which I'd found underneath the shirts.

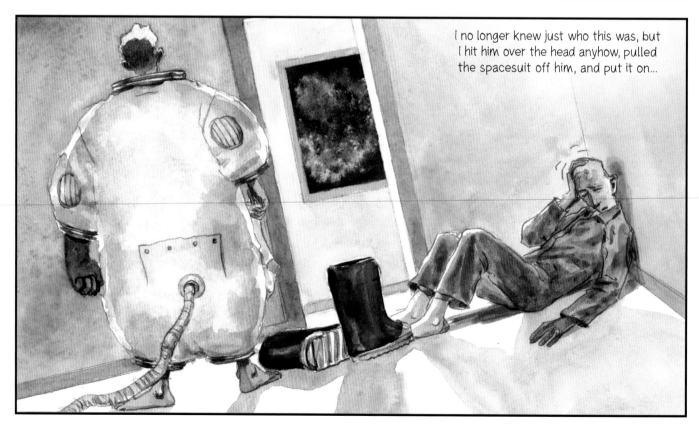

I no longer knew just who this was, but I hit him over the head anyhow, pulled the spacesuit off him, and put it on...

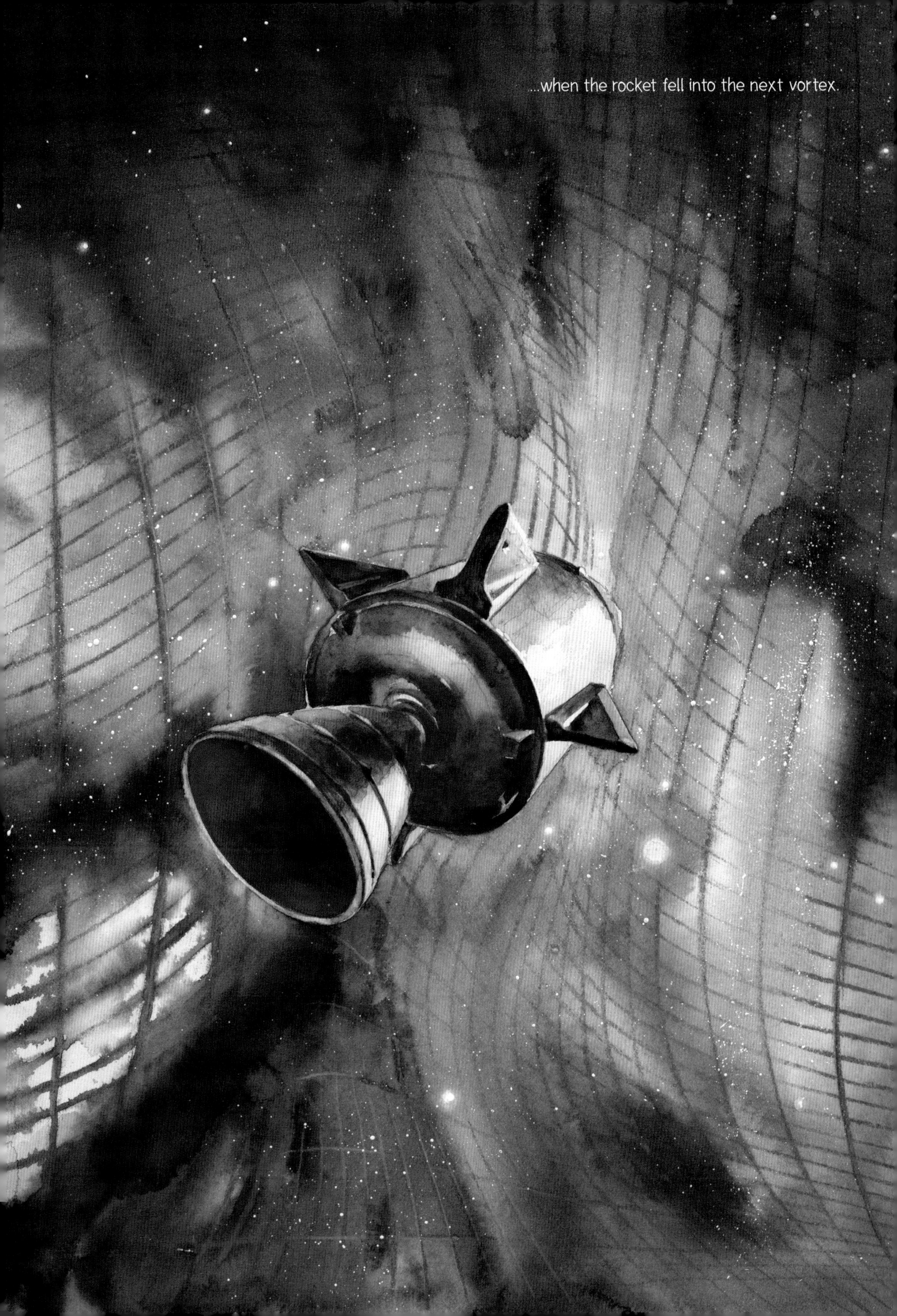
...when the rocket fell into the next vortex.

When I regained consciousness, the cabin was packed with people.

There was barely elbow room.

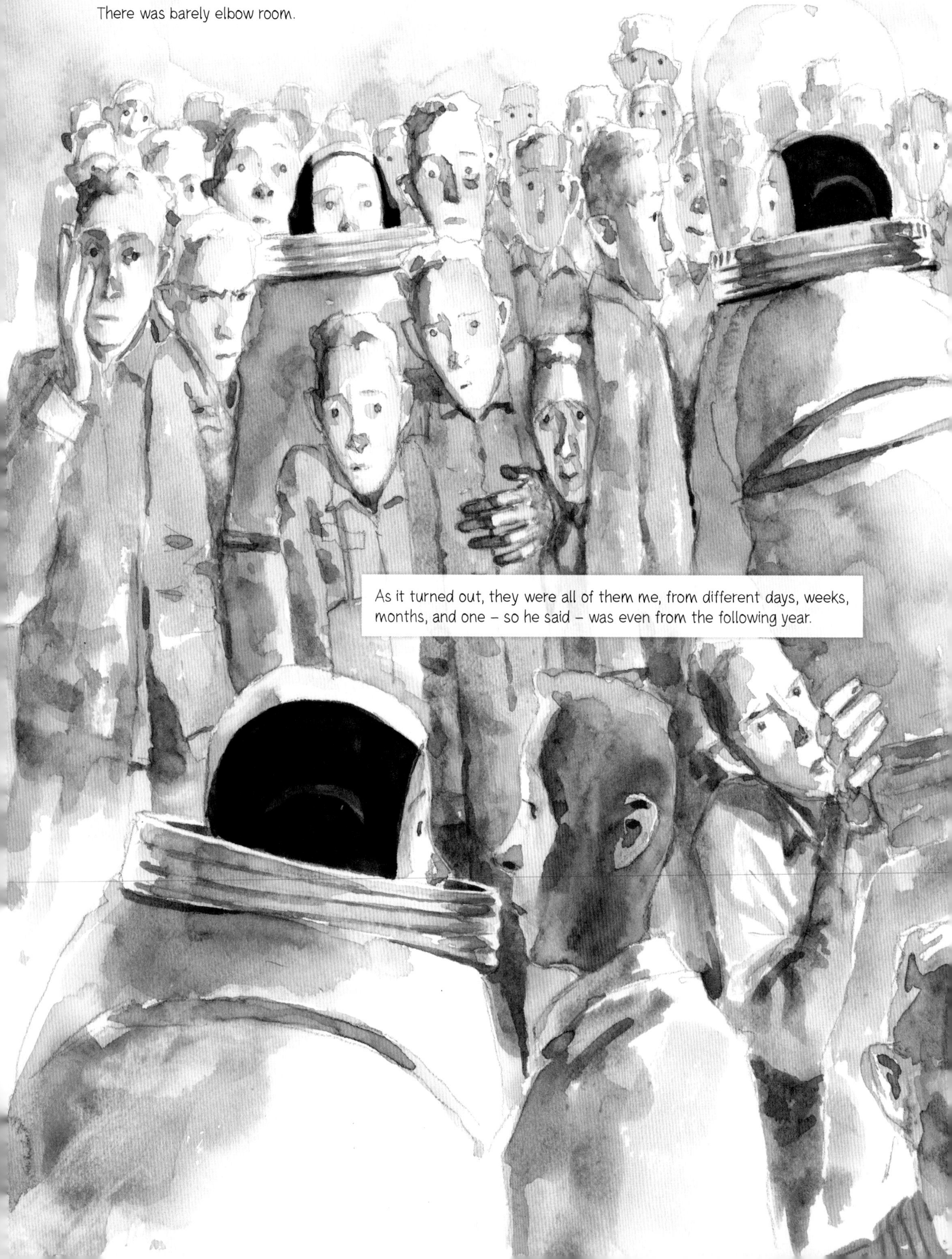
As it turned out, they were all of them me, from different days, weeks, months, and one – so he said – was even from the following year.

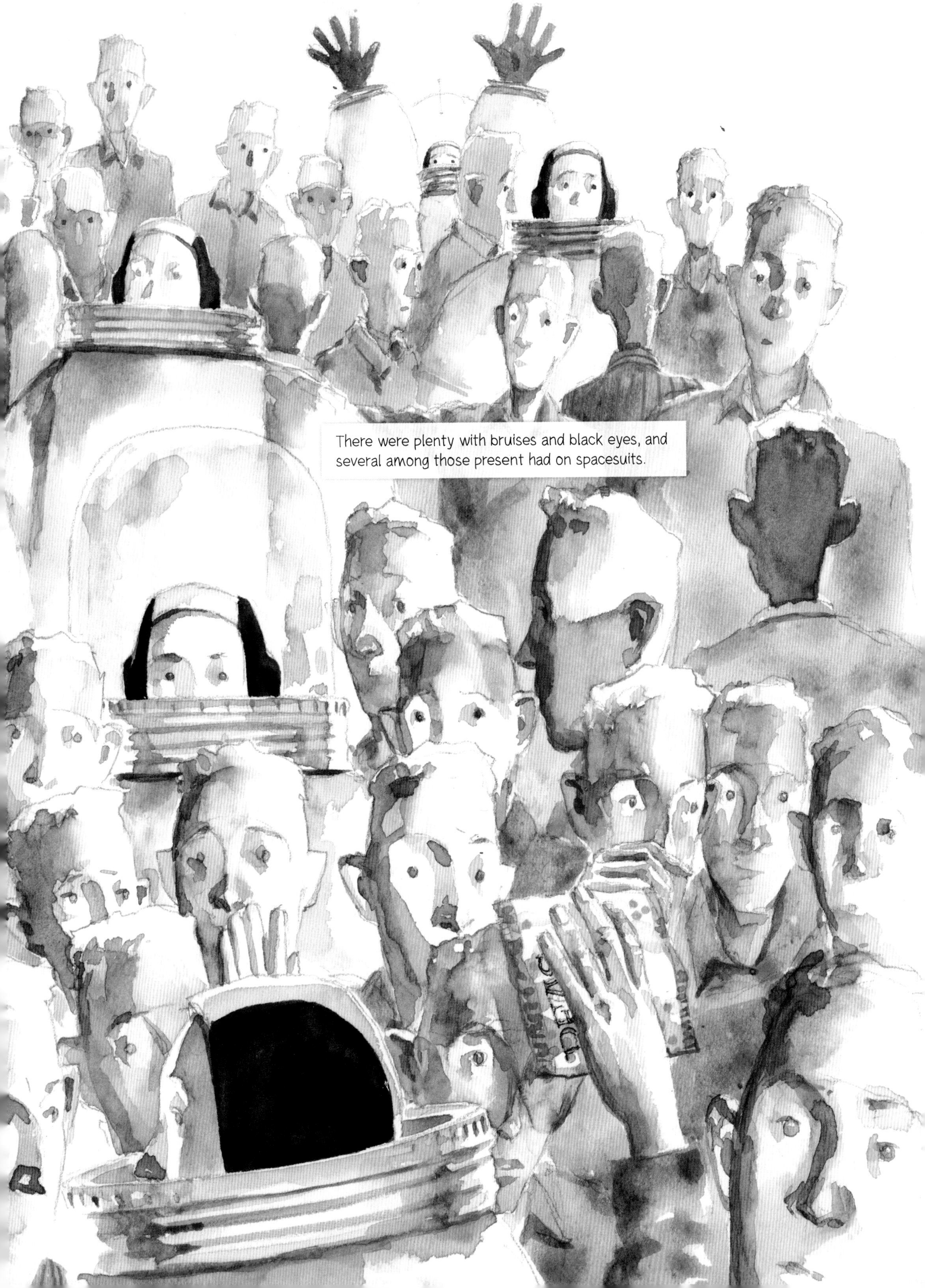
There were plenty with bruises and black eyes, and several among those present had on spacesuits.

But instead of immediately going out through the hatch and repairing the damage, they began to quarrel, argue, bicker, and debate. The problem was, who had hit whom, and when.

The situation was complicated by the fact that there now had appeared morning me's and afternoon me's – I feared that if things went on like this, I would soon be broken into minutes and seconds.

And then, too, the majority of the me's present were lying like mad, so that to this day, I'm not altogether sure whom I hit and who hit me when that whole business took place...

...triangularly, between the Thursday, the Friday, and the Wednesday me's, all of whom I was in turn.

My impression is that because I had lied to the Friday me, pretending to be the Sunday me, I ended up with one more blow than I should have...

...going by the calendar.

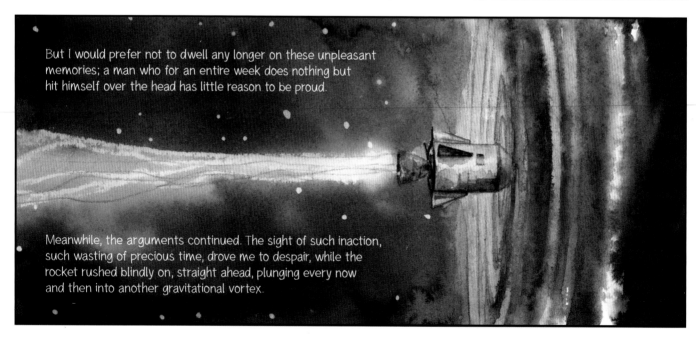

But I would prefer not to dwell any longer on these unpleasant memories; a man who for an entire week does nothing but hit himself over the head has little reason to be proud.

Meanwhile, the arguments continued. The sight of such inaction, such wasting of precious time, drove me to despair, while the rocket rushed blindly on, straight ahead, plunging every now and then into another gravitational vortex.

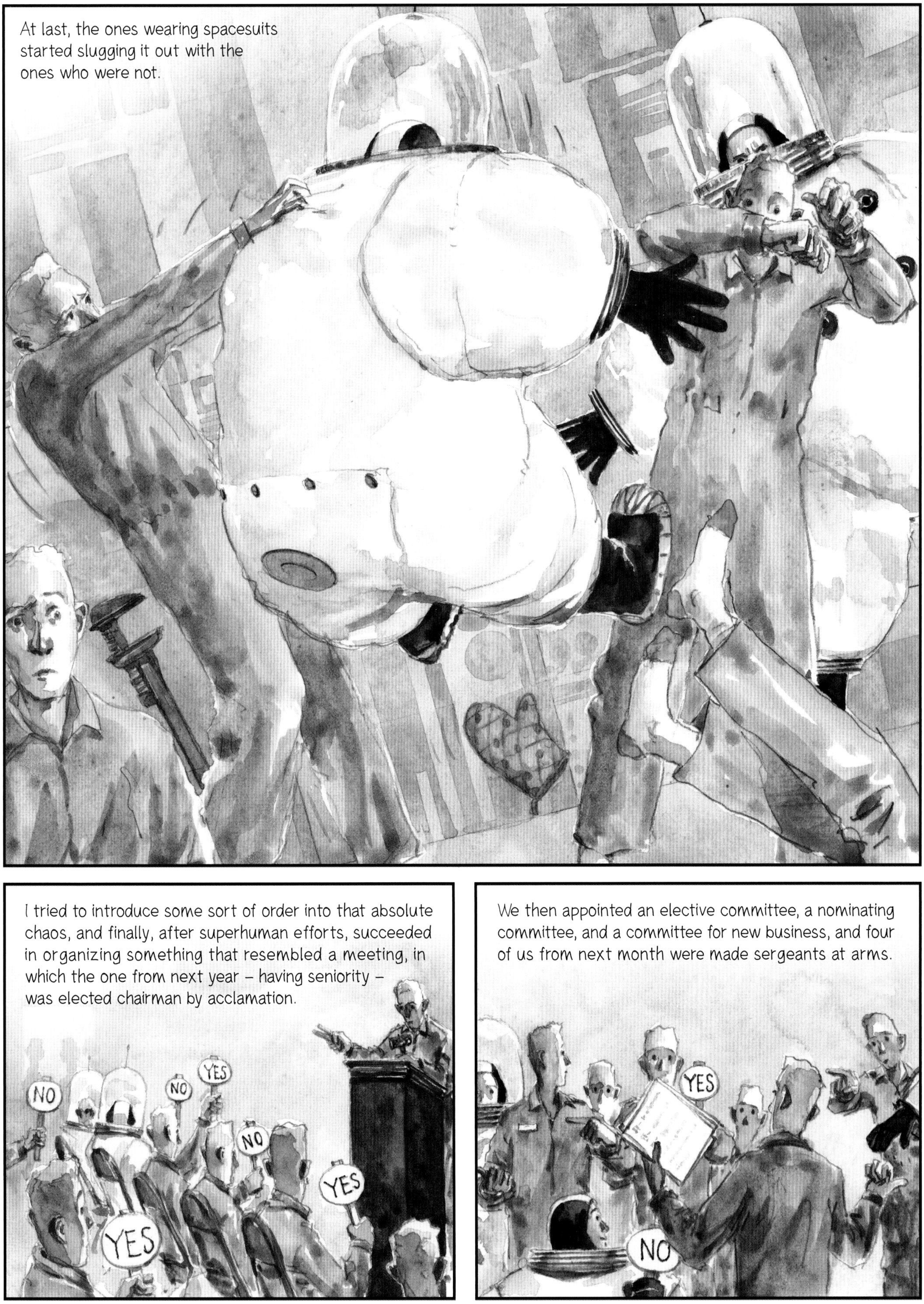
At last, the ones wearing spacesuits started slugging it out with the ones who were not.
I tried to introduce some sort of order into that absolute chaos, and finally, after superhuman efforts, succeeded in organizing something that resembled a meeting, in which the one from next year – having seniority – was elected chairman by acclamation.
NO
NO
YES
NO
YES
YES
We then appointed an elective committee, a nominating committee, and a committee for new business, and four of us from next month were made sergeants at arms.
YES
NO

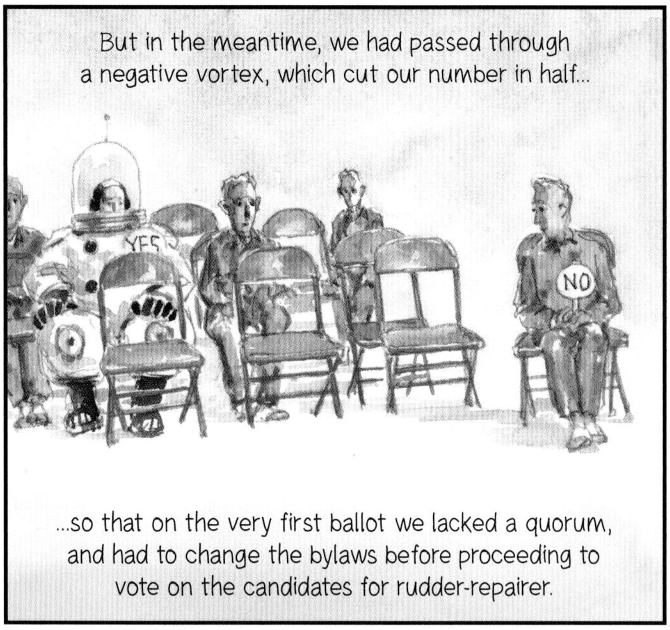
But in the meantime, we had passed through a negative vortex, which cut our number in half...
NO
...so that on the very first ballot we lacked a quorum, and had to change the bylaws before proceeding to vote on the candidates for rudder-repairer.

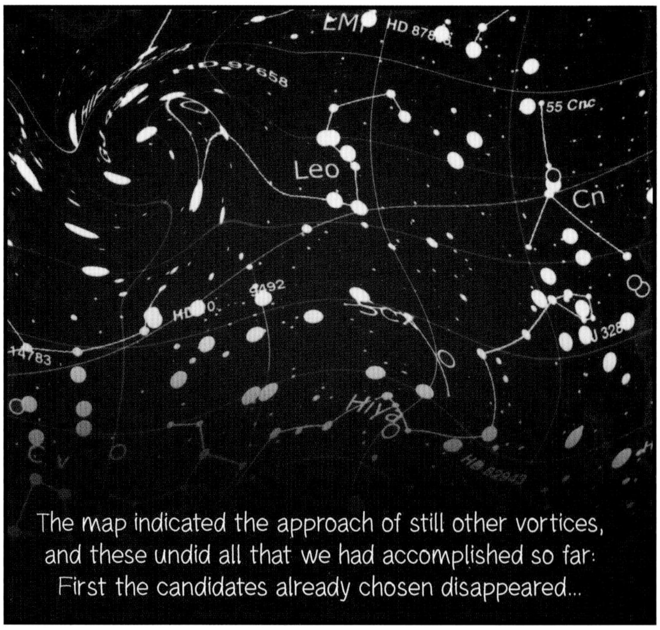
Leo
55 Cnc
The map indicated the approach of still other vortices, and these undid all that we had accomplished so far: First the candidates already chosen disappeared...

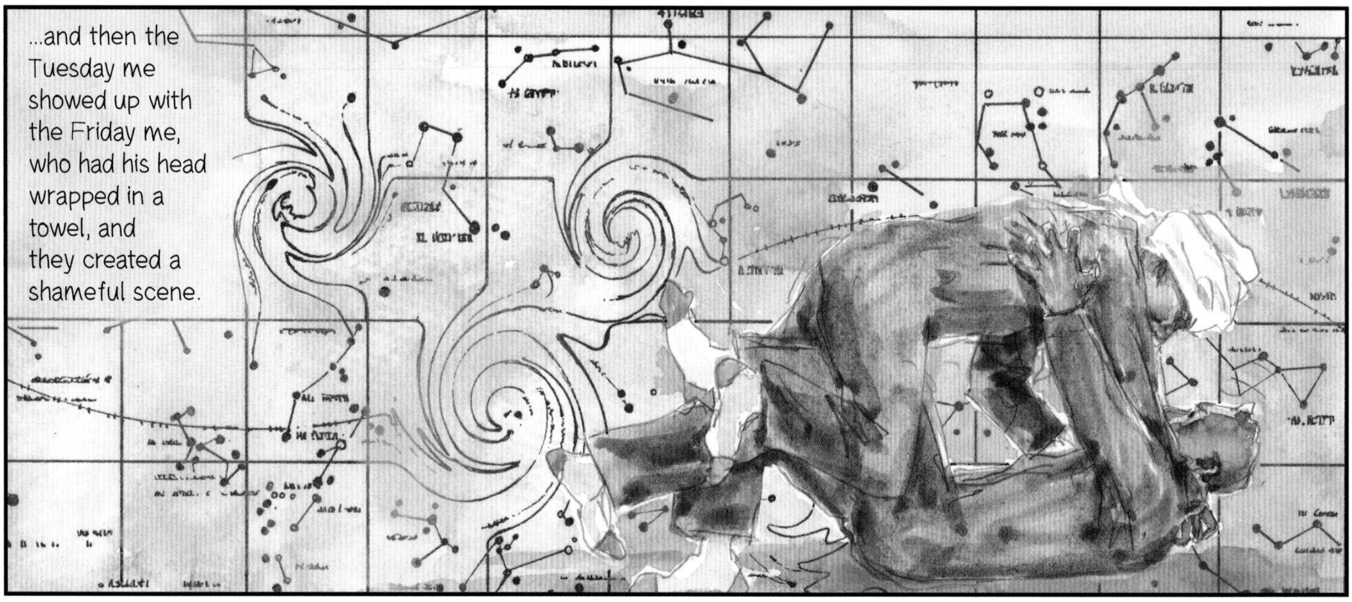
...and then the Tuesday me showed up with the Friday me, who had his head wrapped in a towel, and they created a shameful scene.

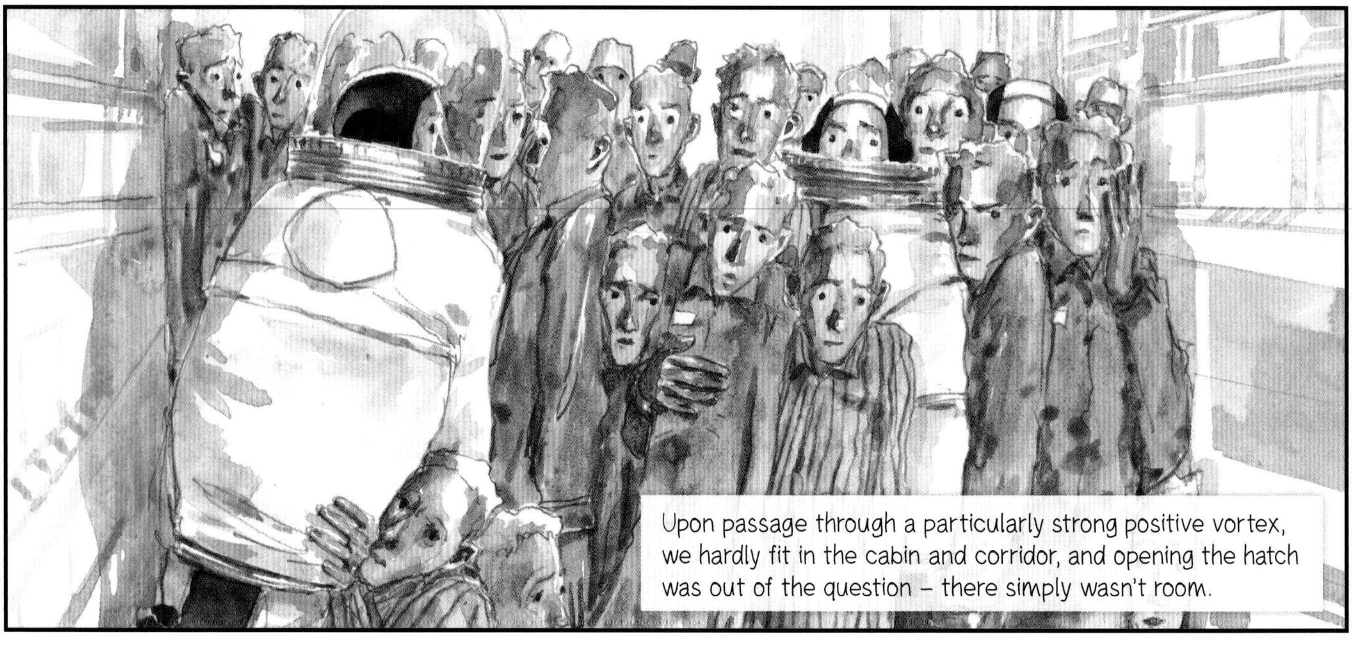
Upon passage through a particularly strong positive vortex, we hardly fit in the cabin and corridor, and opening the hatch was out of the question – there simply wasn't room.

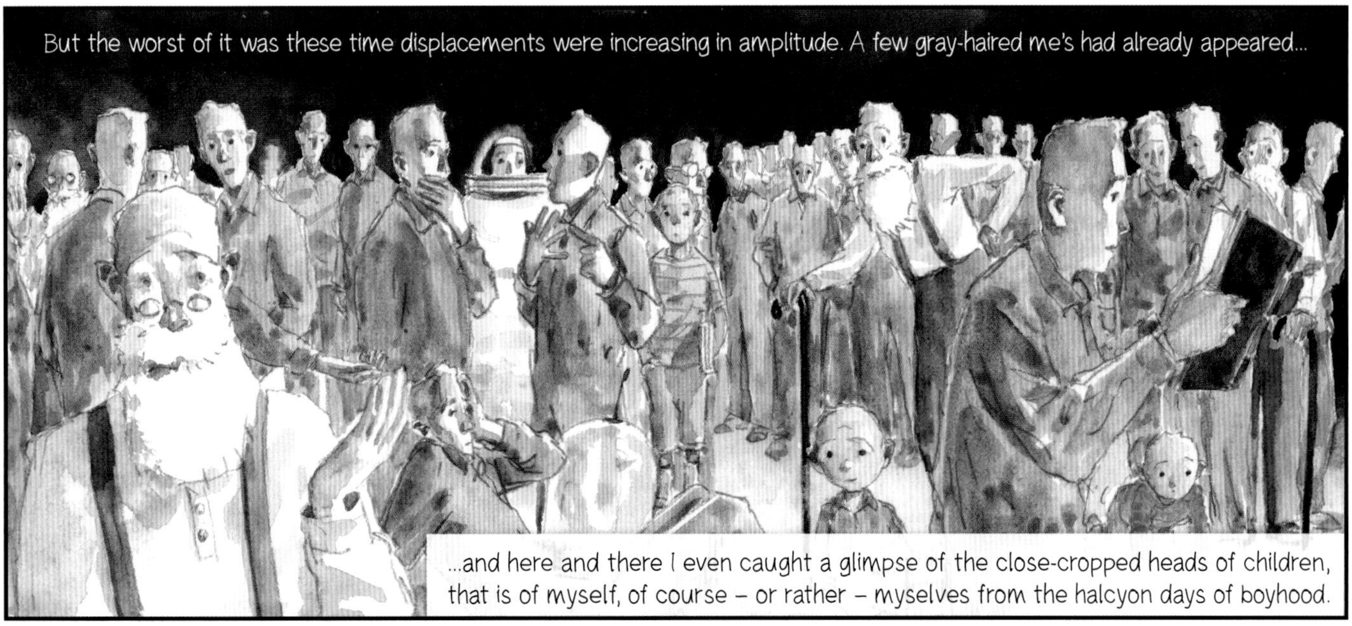
But the worst of it was these time displacements were increasing in amplitude. A few gray-haired me's had already appeared...
...and here and there I even caught a glimpse of the close-cropped heads of children, that is of myself, of course – or rather – myselves from the halcyon days of boyhood.

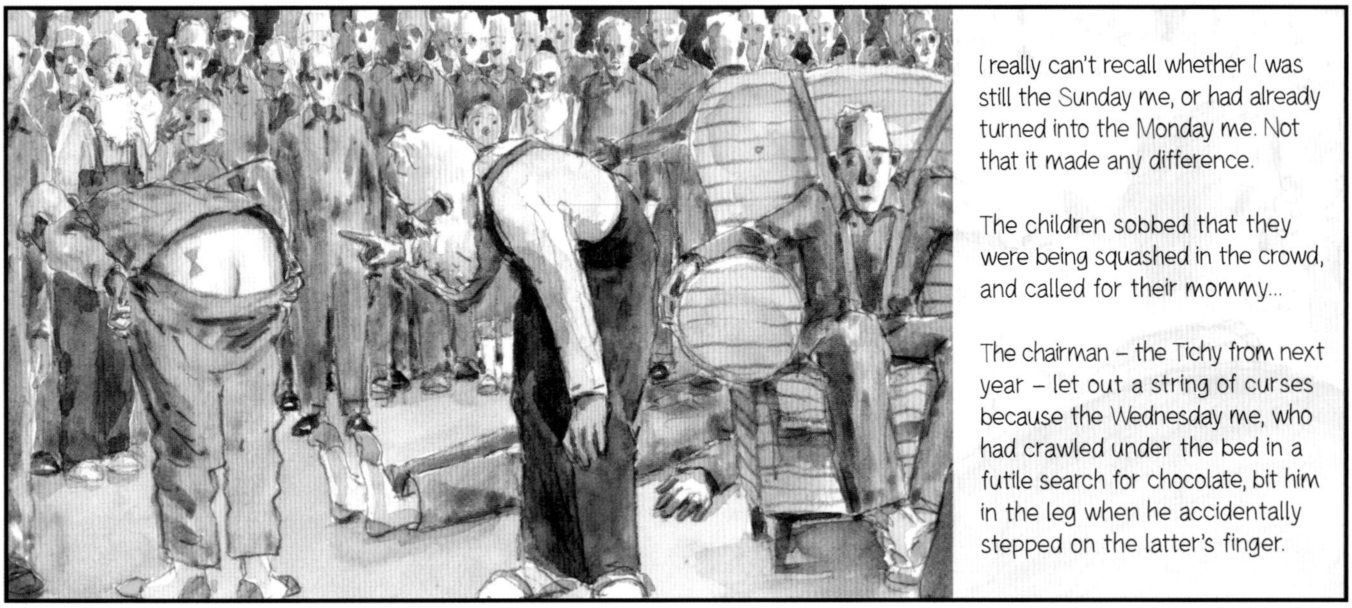
I really can't recall whether I was still the Sunday me, or had already turned into the Monday me. Not that it made any difference.
The children sobbed that they were being squashed in the crowd, and called for their mommy...
The chairman – the Tichy from next year – let out a string of curses because the Wednesday me, who had crawled under the bed in a futile search for chocolate, bit him in the leg when he accidentally stepped on the latter's finger.

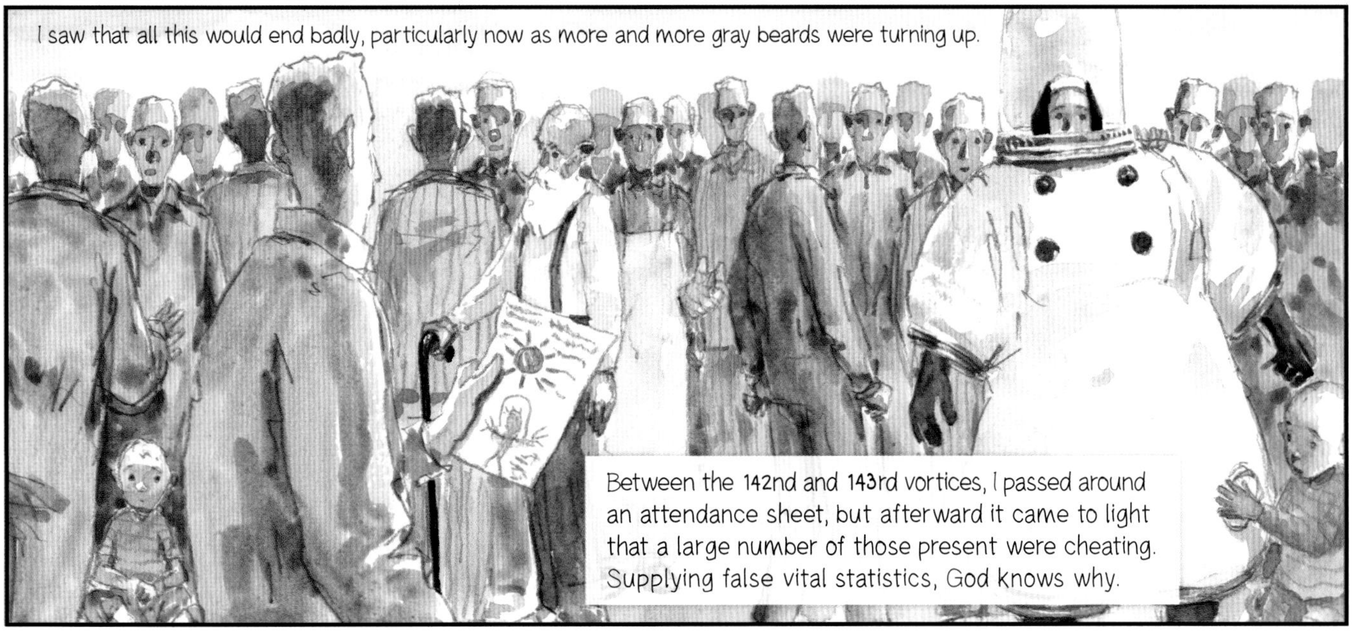
I saw that all this would end badly, particularly now as more and more gray beards were turning up.
Between the 142nd and 143rd vortices, I passed around an attendance sheet, but afterward it came to light that a large number of those present were cheating. Supplying false vital statistics, God knows why.

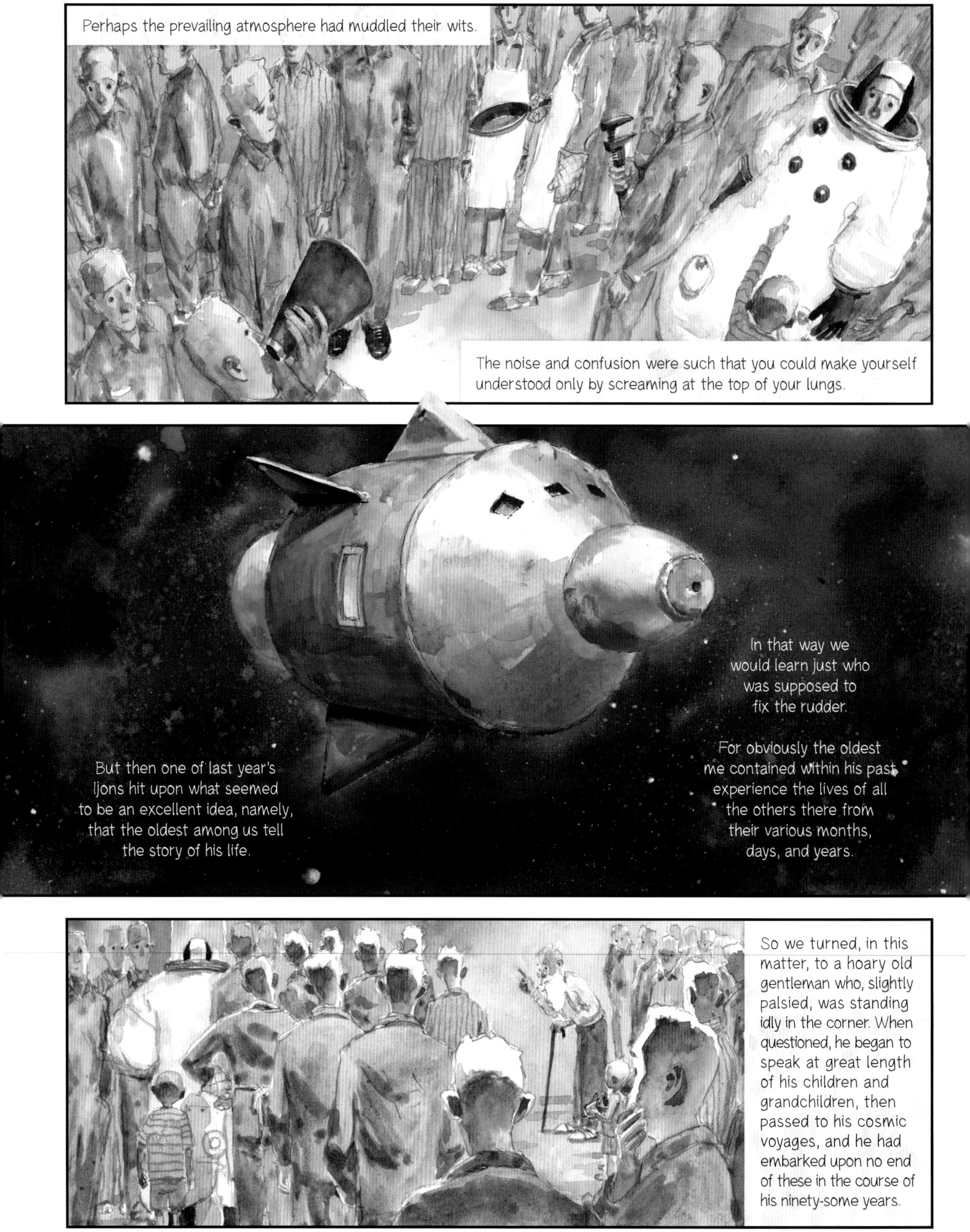
Perhaps the prevailing atmosphere had muddled their wits.
The noise and confusion were such that you could make yourself understood only by screaming at the top of your lungs.
But then one of last year's Ijons hit upon what seemed to be an excellent idea, namely, that the oldest among us tell the story of his life.
In that way we would learn just who was supposed to fix the rudder.
For obviously the oldest me contained within his past experience the lives of all the others there from their various months, days, and years.
So we turned, in this matter, to a hoary old gentleman who, slightly palsied, was standing idly in the corner. When questioned, he began to speak at great length of his children and grandchildren, then passed to his cosmic voyages, and he had embarked upon no end of these in the course of his ninety-some years.

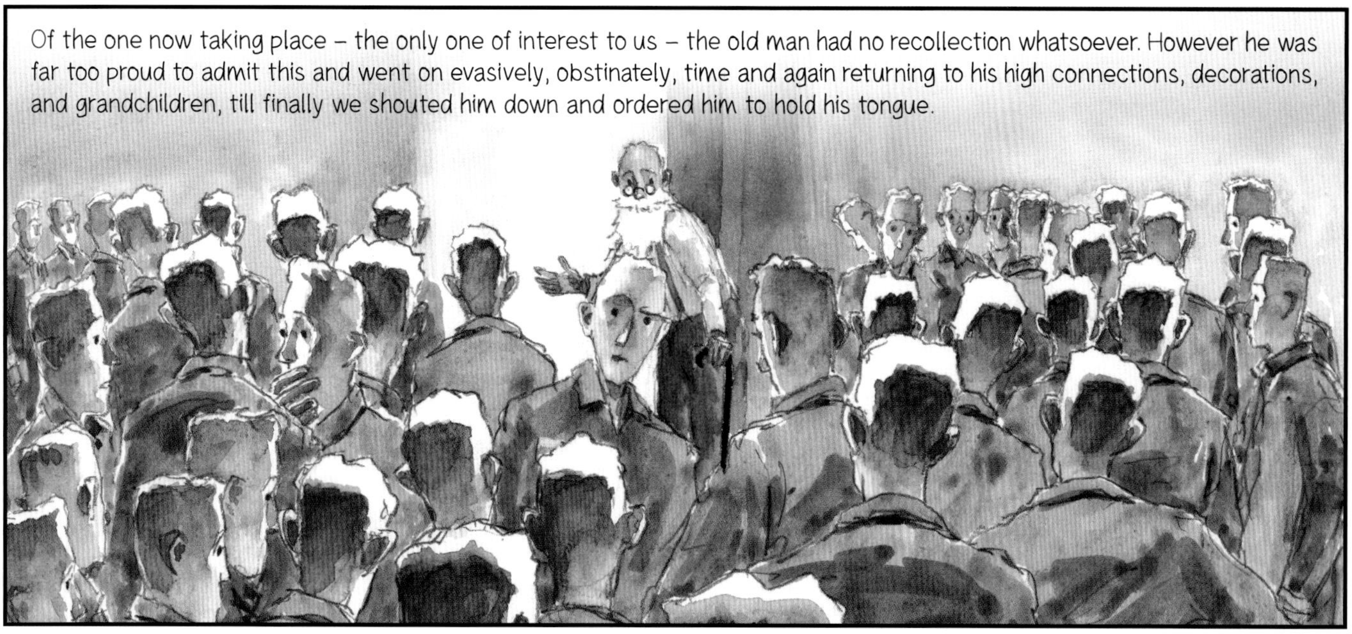
Of the one now taking place – the only one of interest to us – the old man had no recollection whatsoever. However he was far too proud to admit this and went on evasively, obstinately, time and again returning to his high connections, decorations, and grandchildren, till finally we shouted him down and ordered him to hold his tongue.

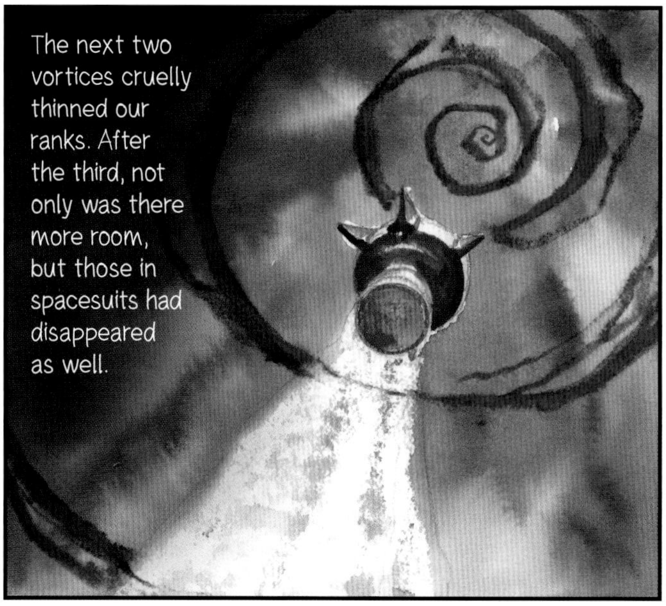
The next two vortices cruelly thinned our ranks. After the third, not only was there more room, but those in spacesuits had disappeared as well.

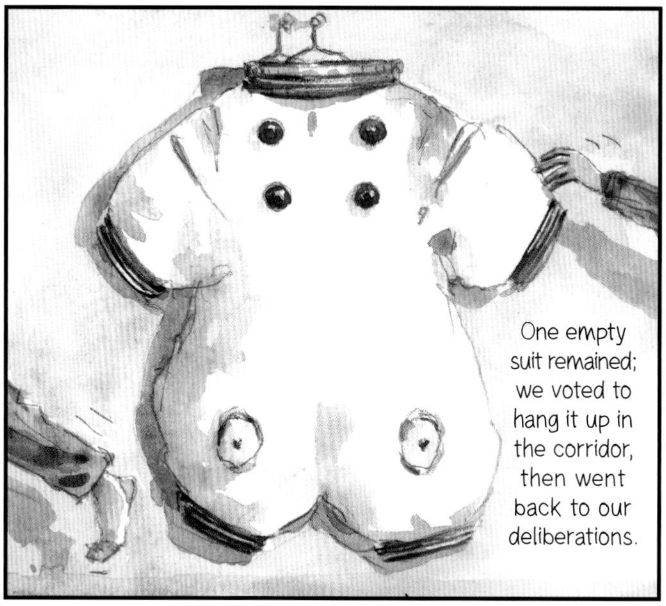
One empty suit remained; we voted to hang it up in the corridor, then went back to our deliberations.

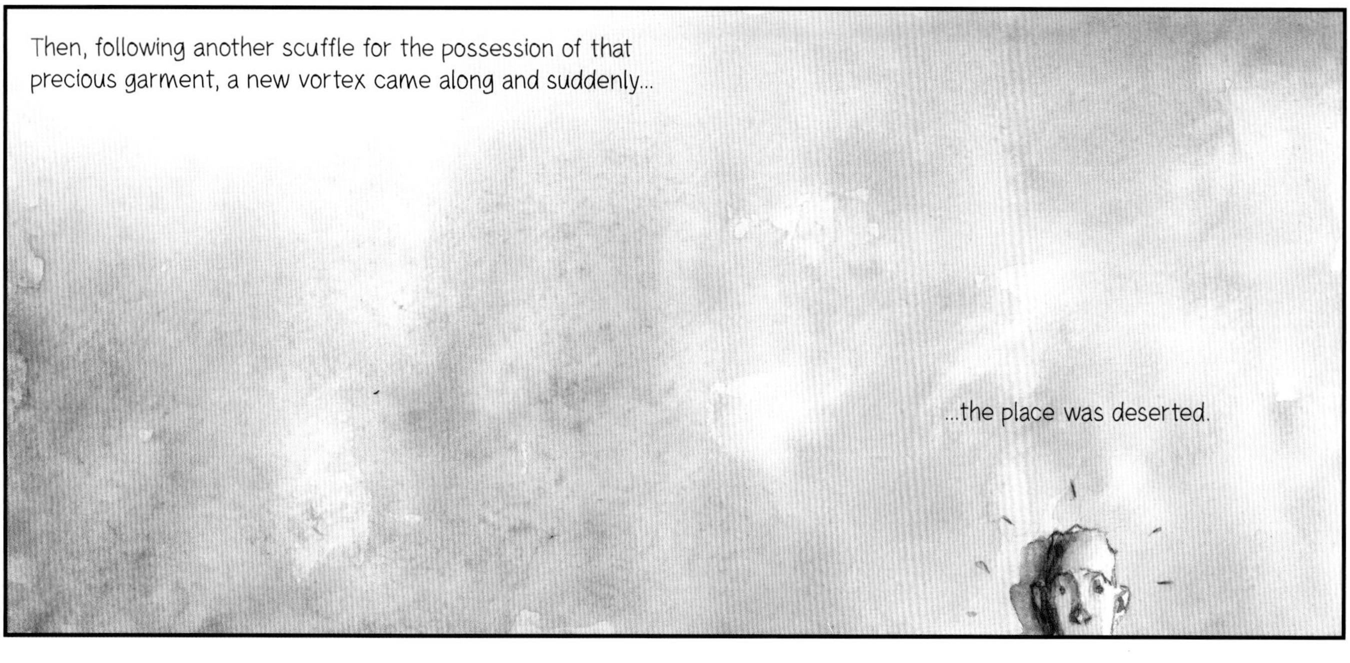
Then, following another scuffle for the possession of that precious garment, a new vortex came along and suddenly...
...the place was deserted.

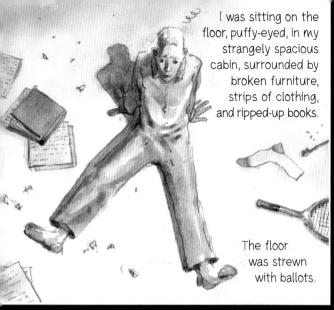

I was sitting on the floor, puffy-eyed, in my strangely spacious cabin, surrounded by broken furniture, strips of clothing, and ripped-up books.

The floor was strewn with ballots.

According to the map, I had now passed through the entire zone of gravitational vortices.

No longer able to count on duplication, and thus no longer able to correct the damage, I fell into numb despair.

About an hour later, I looked out in the corridor and discovered, to my great surprise, that the spacesuit was missing.

But then I vaguely remembered – yes – right before that last vortex, two little boys sneaked out into the corridor.

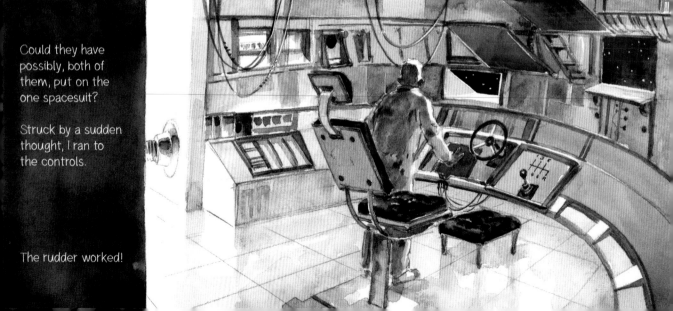

Could they have possibly, both of them, put on the one spacesuit?

Struck by a sudden thought, I ran to the controls.

The rudder worked!

So then, those little tykes had fixed it after all, while we adults were stuck in endless disagreements.

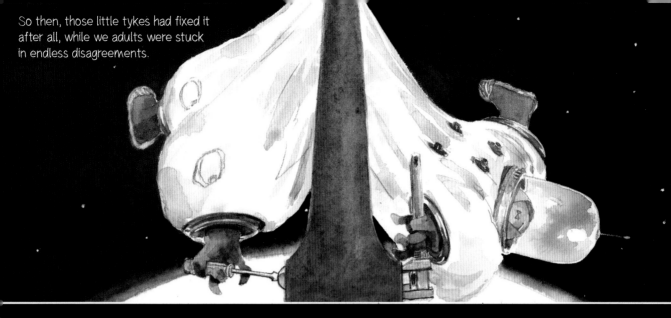

I imagine that one of them placed his arms in the sleeves of the suit, and the other in the pants; that way, they could have tightened the nut and bolt with wrenches at the same time, working on either side of the rudder.

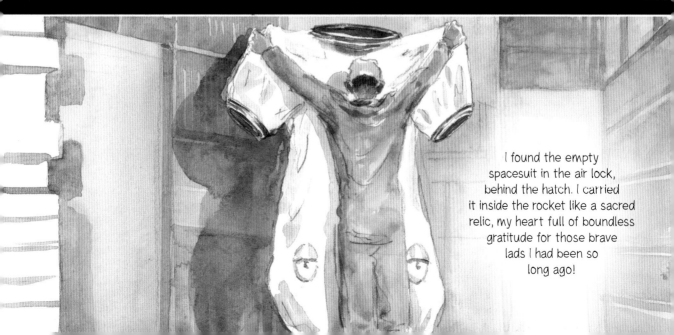

I found the empty spacesuit in the air lock, behind the hatch. I carried it inside the rocket like a sacred relic, my heart full of boundless gratitude for those brave lads I had been so long ago!

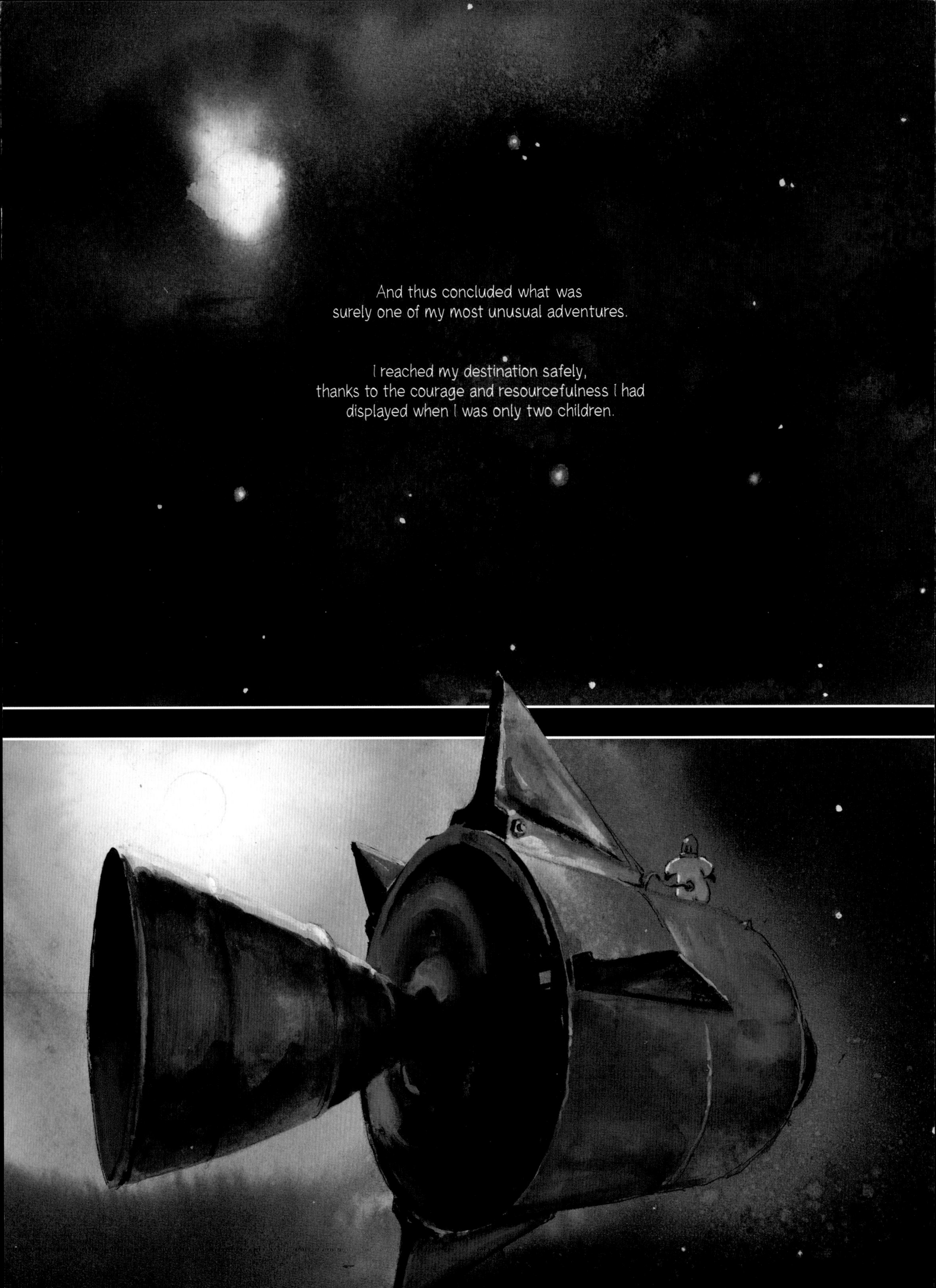
And thus concluded what was surely one of my most unusual adventures.
I reached my destination safely, thanks to the courage and resourcefulness I had displayed when I was only two children.

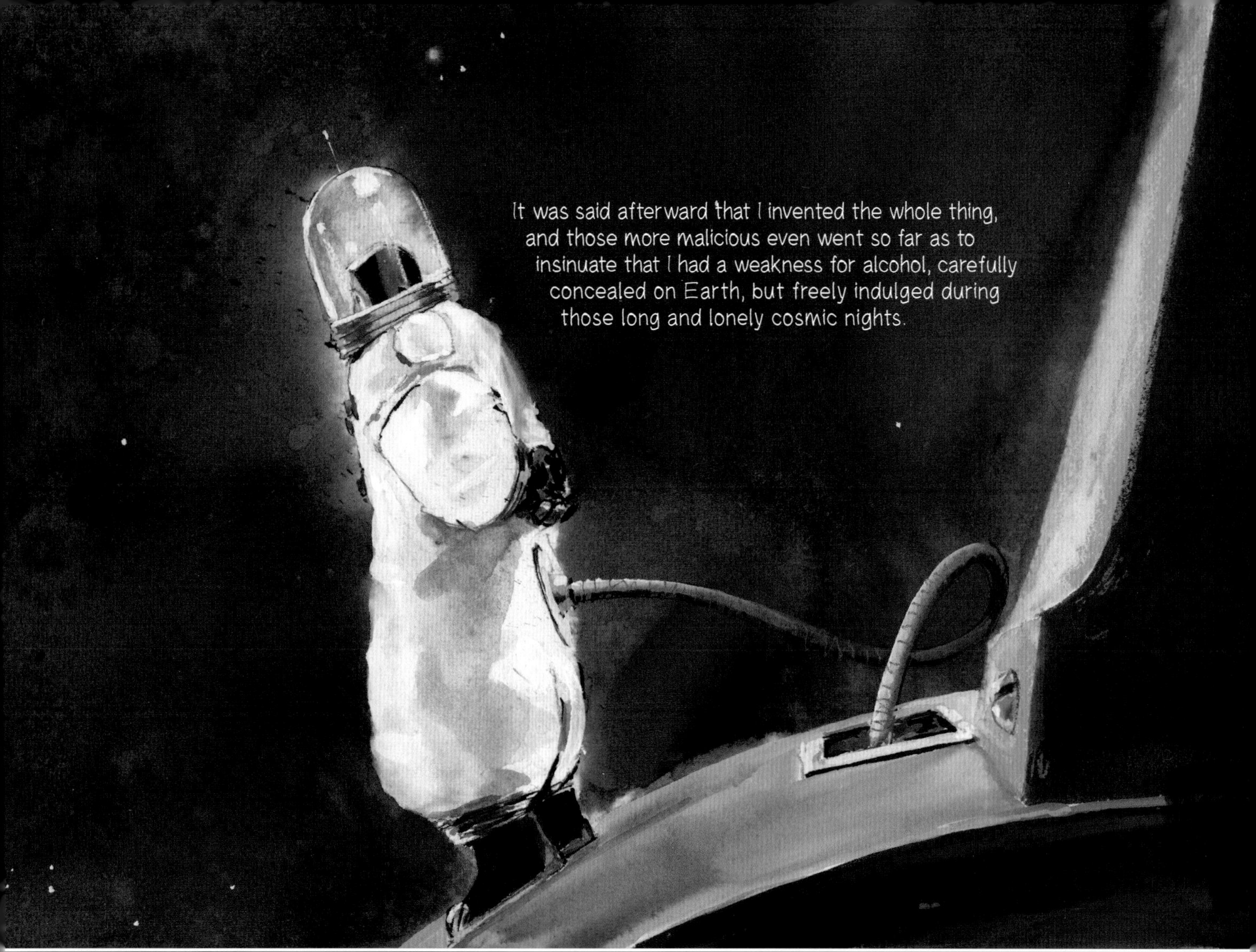
It was said afterward that I invented the whole thing, and those more malicious even went so far as to insinuate that I had a weakness for alcohol, carefully concealed on Earth, but freely indulged during those long and lonely cosmic nights.

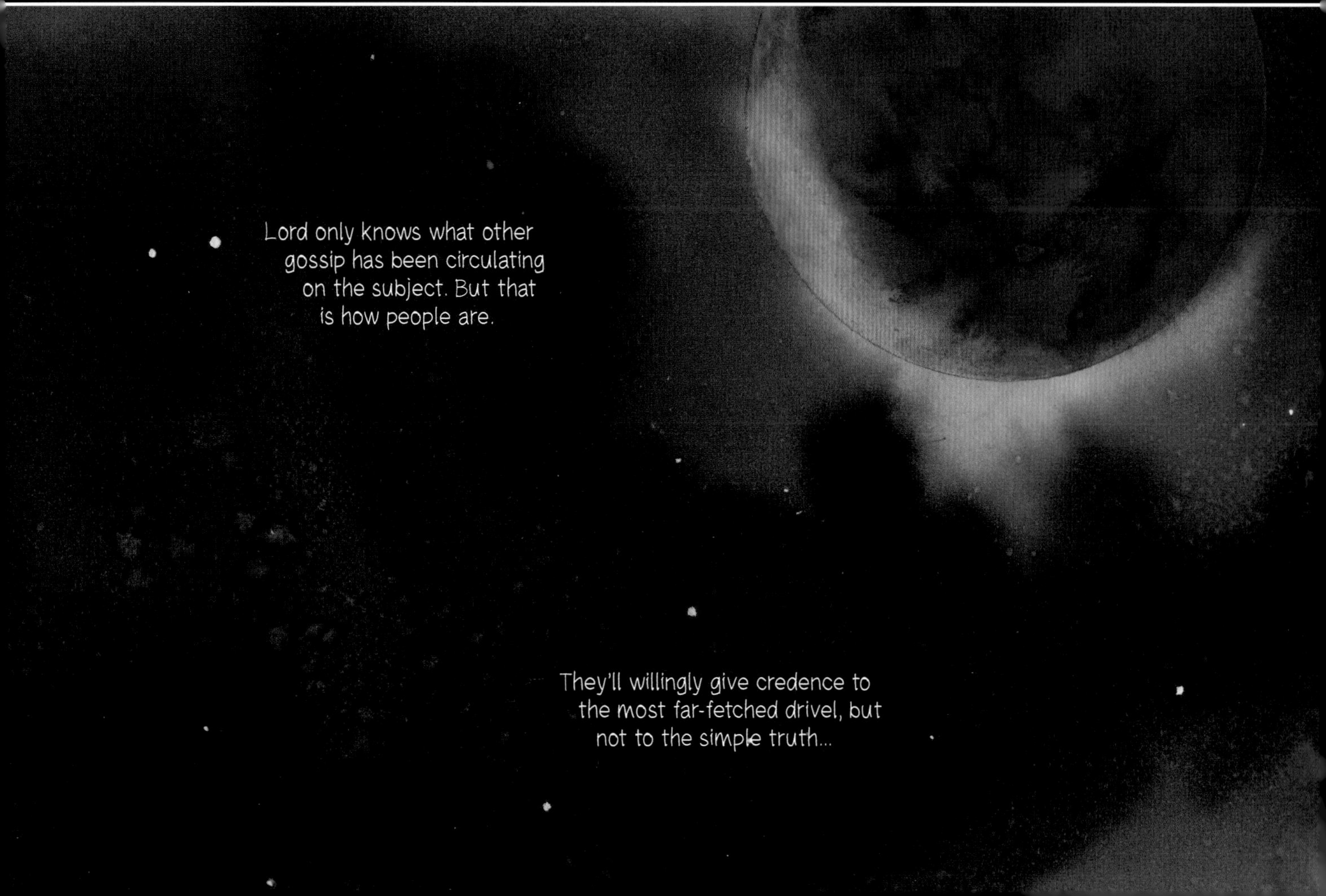
Lord only knows what other gossip has been circulating on the subject. But that is how people are.
They'll willingly give credence to the most far-fetched drivel, but not to the simple truth...

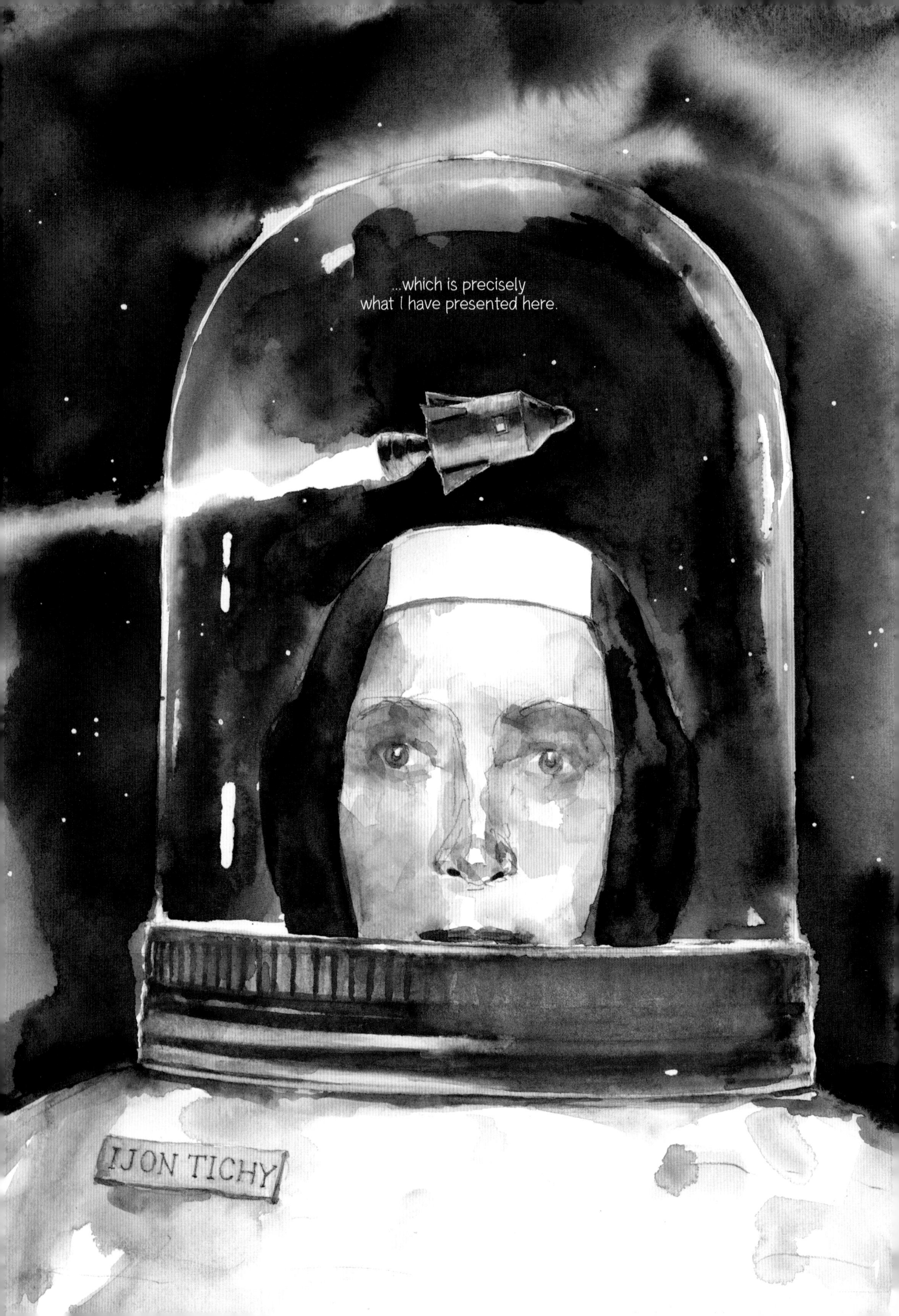
...which is precisely
what I have presented here.
IJON TICHY

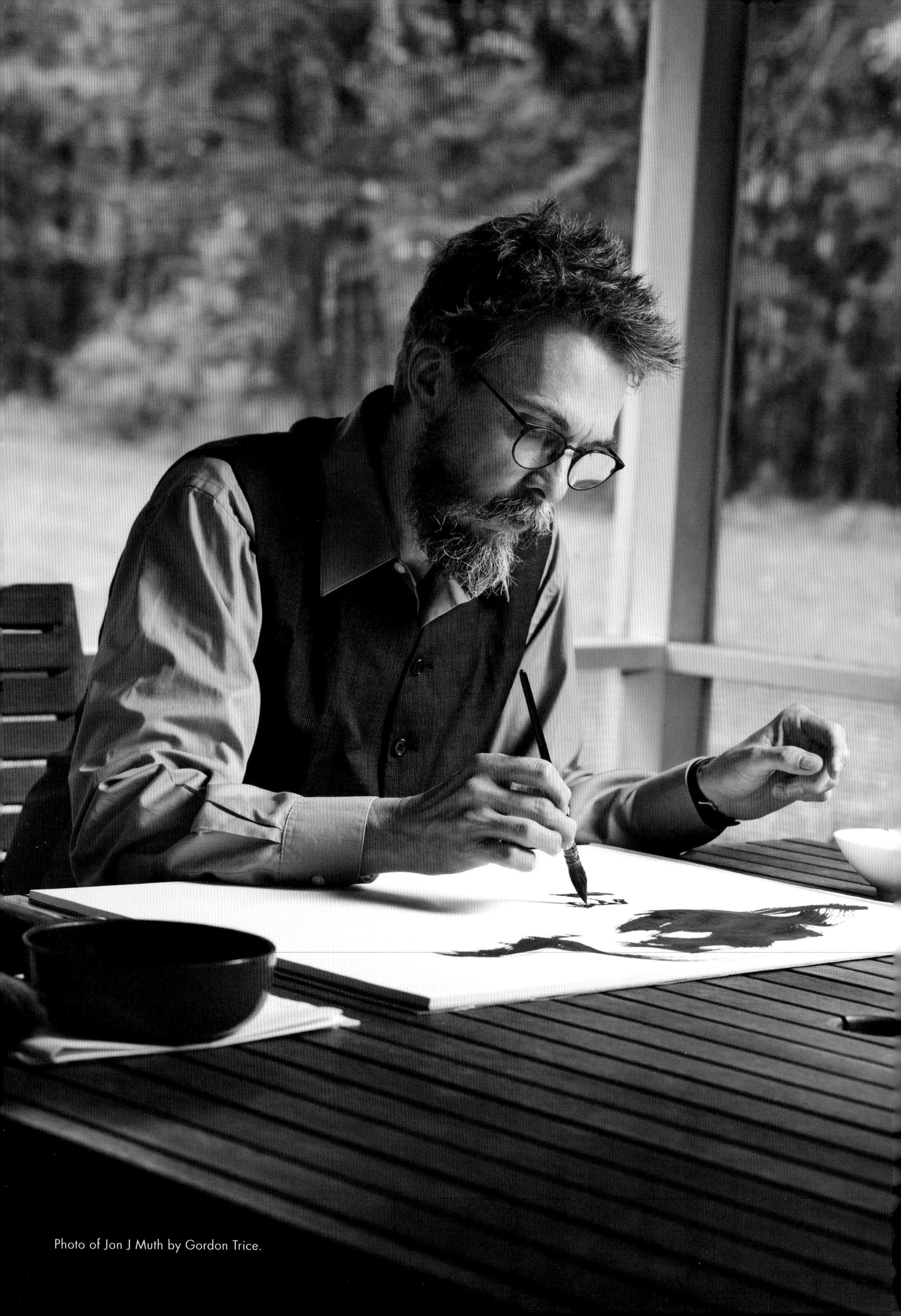

Photo of Jon J Muth by Gordon Trice.

ADAPTER'S NOTE

I write and illustrate children's picture books. I have always loved the form of words and pictures together. Before I created picture books, I worked in comics.

By 1992 I had done *Moonshadow*, and I had written and illustrated a graphic novel of *Dracula* and *The Mythology of an Abandoned City*. At that time in America, comics and graphic novels were still dominated by superheroes. The form itself had not yet been validated as a respected literary vehicle. It seemed obvious to me that comics were an intriguing way to examine and explore any aspect of life that prose or film could. After all, Art Spiegelman's *Maus* had happened! I dreamed of working with a writer that matched where I wanted to go. The writers I was most excited by were: Graham Greene, John Fowles, Edith Pearlman, John C. Gardner, Ursula K. Le Guin, Stanislaw Lem . . .

I decided to write to Stanislaw Lem, never really expecting any response. I remember the feeling at the time was like sending a message in a bottle. And Lem wrote back and said, "OK. What would you like to do?"

I had read science fiction throughout my childhood. You could find secondhand paperbacks for fifteen cents at the pharmacy near my house. All my lunch money went toward books. Leaving the store with a grocery bag full, I learned to love Bradbury, Ellison, Philip K. Dick, Asimov, and Bester. Then I found a copy of *Solaris*. I was accustomed to visiting other worlds, but this book was . . . another way of thinking about everything.

As a science-fiction writer, Lem wrote books with an astonishing diversity of forms. They could be entertaining, full of wisdom, silly, mysterious, and often quite dark. Uniquely he could bridge the themes that were familiar in science fiction, like cosmic exploration, then demonstrate how the true "stranger in a strange land" is us — in that our motivations are so non-transparent to ourselves as to be alien. Much of Lem's writing explores how oblivious we are to our limits. Sometimes our limited perception creates tragedy or horror, as in *Solaris*, and sometimes comedy, as in *The Seventh Voyage*. I thought about Lem's question for a while: "What would you like to do?" I decided on a story with his space explorer, Ijon Tichy.

Utopian visions of the future are favorite targets of Lem's satire, and the stories of space traveler Ijon Tichy run from the profound to the ridiculous. *The Seventh Voyage* is a time-travel parody that first appeared in English in *The Star Diaries* (1976), a collection of short stories about Tichy's space adventures. His adventures continued in *Memoirs of a Space Traveler* (1982), *The Futurological Congress* (1974), and *Peace on Earth* (1987).

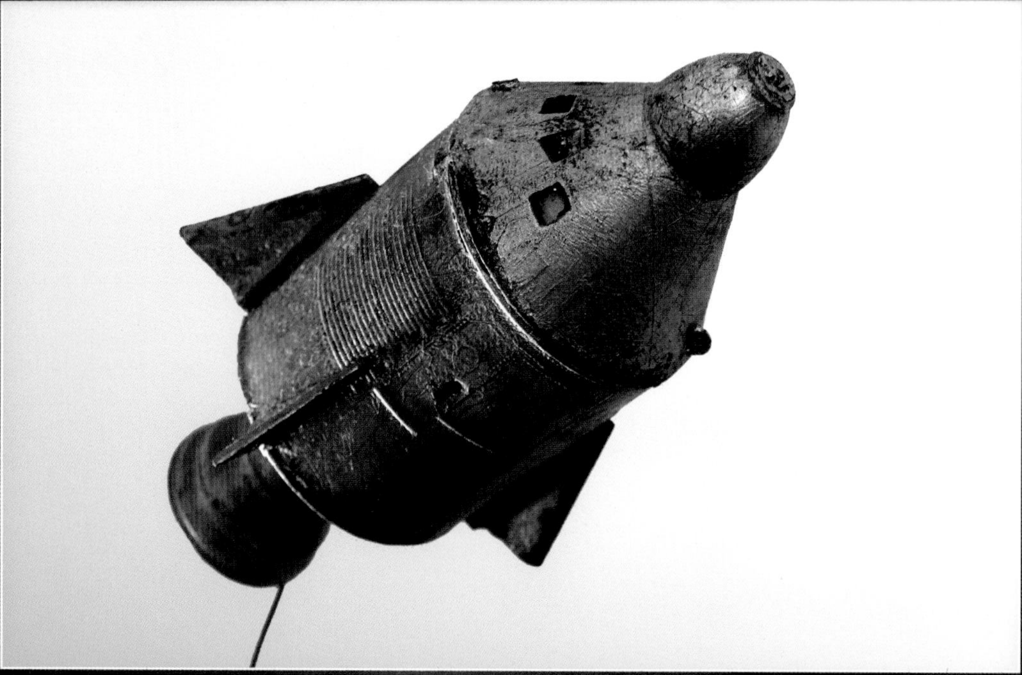

Stanislaw Lem, a Polish author, was born in 1921 in Lviv (which is now in Ukraine). His father and uncle were doctors, and Lem trained as a physician at Lviv University. During the World War II occupation, all universities were closed. Lem survived working as an auto mechanic and a welder. Much of Lem's writing was done under communism, when censorship was strict and criticism of official doctrines had powerful consequences. Lem often used tricks to encrypt the political or cultural criticism in his books. Humor helped make it easier to get his ideas published.

In 2005, my Scholastic Art Director, David Saylor, told me they were starting a new graphic novel imprint called "Graphix," and was there anything I wanted to do in that form? "Well," I said, "there is this one story . . ."

To begin the book, I made several sculptural models. I often do sculptures of characters before drawing a book, so I can see how light will fall over a figure. I made a pose-able puppet of Tichy like the kind you might use in a stop-motion film. My brother, who has a "Stan Laurel" quality, served as the early inspiration for my drawings of Ijon Tichy. I created Tichy's spaceship, careful not to let the technology look too designed. Since Lem was a mechanic I wanted the tools and the interior to feel like a garage. The inside of the ship would be bigger than the outside to emphasize the crowding in of multiple Tichys.

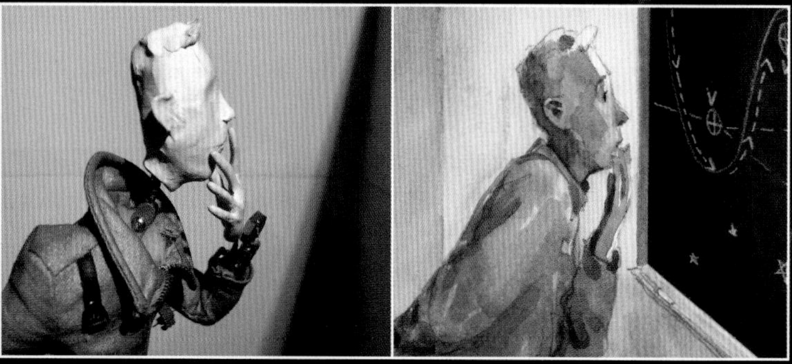

Here is an example of how the sculptural model of Ijon Tichy was transformed into a finished painting.

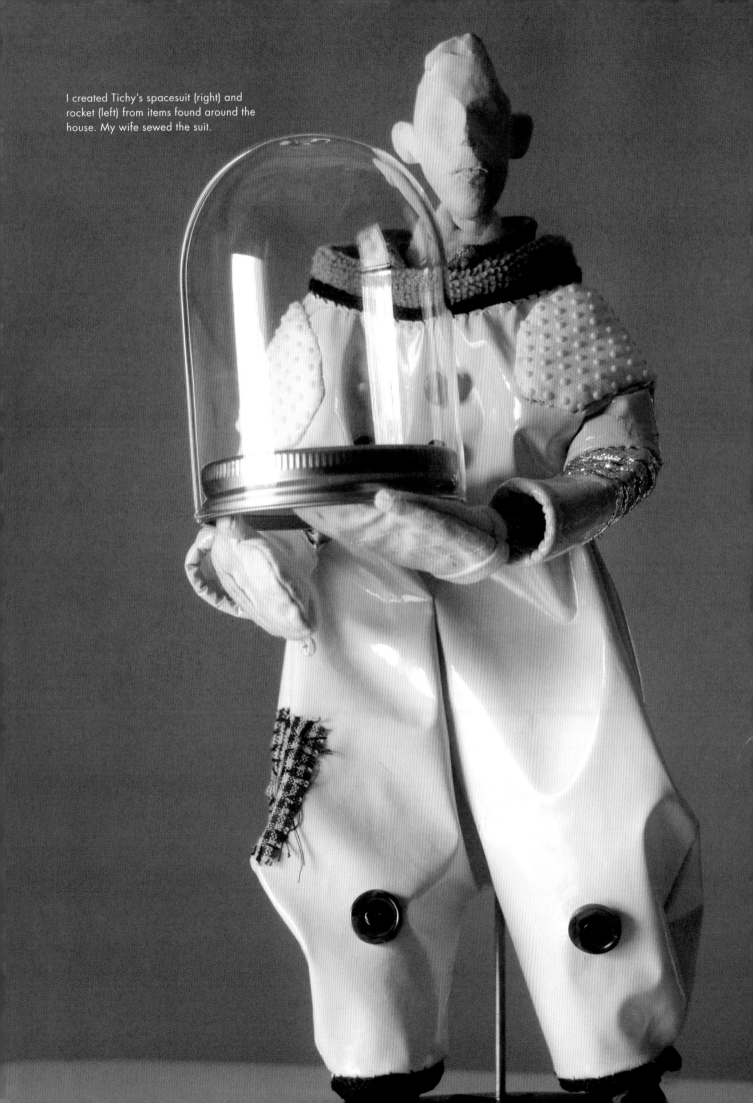

I created Tichy's spacesuit (right) and rocket (left) from items found around the house. My wife sewed the suit.

Oil painting of Stanislaw Lem, 1989, by Jon J Muth from a photo by Boleslaw Lutoslawski.

Lem wrote about Ijon Tichy throughout his career. Starting in the early 1950s, the character continued to fascinate Lem into the 1980s. The stories weren't written in the order of the voyage numbers. *The Twenty-Second Voyage* was written long before *The Seventh Voyage*. Tichy's adventures, like Lem's fiction, ranged from slapstick to deep introspections about religion or the nature of consciousness. Each new world Tichy visits is a stepping-off point for Lem to make a comment about the human condition, and to amuse the reader with observations about the ludicrous social, political, or personal foibles we all are part of.

While I was working on *The Seventh Voyage*, Lem's story became more and more vivid. The simple overarching absurdity of the premise gave way to something deeper. Ijon Tichy (who always managed to get in his own way) was his own worst enemy — as I have been in taking so long to create this book.

I'm happy Graphix is home to *The Seventh Voyage*. And I am grateful and excited to introduce Stanislaw Lem's voice to this medium.

Jon J Muth
APRIL 7, 2019

STANISLAW LEM (1921–2006) was a Polish author from Lviv (now Ukraine). He began his studies in medicine, which were interrupted by WWII. Lem worked as a car mechanic and a welder, and was a member of the resistance, fighting against the Germans. With false papers, he was able to conceal his Jewish identity, and thus avoided the concentration camps. After the war, he completed his medical degree, and while working as a research assistant he began his prodigious literary career.

Lem became one of the greatest writers of the twentieth century — "a virtuoso storyteller" according to the *New York Times*, whose books "convey the sense of a mind hovering above the boundaries of the human condition". While most of his works are science fiction, he was a master of a number of genres and styles from satire to philosophy. Lem's books have been translated into forty-one languages and have sold over thirty million copies. His most famous novel, *Solaris*, was made into a film in 1971 by Andrei Tarkovsky, and remade in 2002 by Steven Soderbergh.

Ijon Tichy is the main character and narrator of *The Star Diaries*, *The Futurological Congress*, *Inspection at the Scene of a Crime*, and *Peace on Earth*. He was one of Lem's favorite characters. Tichy does not have a family, hence he usually travels. He is frequently compared to Munchausen and Gulliver.

To learn more about Stanislaw Lem go to his official website: english.lem.pl

JON J MUTH is renowned in the world of graphic novels. He won an Eisner Award for his paintings in the graphic novel *The Mystery Play* by Grant Morrison, and he has partnered with Neil Gaiman on *The Sandman: The Wake*, Walter and Louise Simonson on *Havok & Wolverine: Meltdown*, and J. M. DeMatteis on *Moonshadow* and *Silver Surfer*.

His many highly acclaimed picture books include his Caldecott Honor Book *Zen Shorts*, and his book *The Three Questions*, which is based on a short story by Leo Tolstoy and was called "quietly life-changing" by the *New York Times*. His books have been translated into more than fifteen languages and are cherished by readers of all ages. Jon lives in New York with his wife and their four children.

MICHAEL KANDEL'S working relationship with Stanislaw Lem began with a student's fan letter to his favorite author — and flourished into a successful author-translator collaboration of two decades. Kandel is notable for capturing Lem's style, which is marked by rich wordplay, puns, and unconventional language.

Mr. Kandel says: "I believe that Stanislaw Lem, had he lived to see it, would have been extremely pleased with Jon J Muth's graphic novel version of 'The Seventh Voyage' from *The Star Diaries*. Muth's charming, playful touches fit the story perfectly. So delightful and so funny! Applause for the artist!"

ACKNOWLEDGMENTS

THANK YOU TO MY HEROIC TEAM OF SPACEFARERS!

Dianne Hess

David Saylor

My right-hand man, Allen Spiegel, without whom
I wouldn't have nearly as much adventure in my life.

Michael Kandel for his generosity and genius.

Franz Rottensteiner, his timely connection to SL made this book possible.

Thank you also to Phil Falco and Shivana Sookdeo for a great design.

Thanks to Arthur Fraude for access to the Ballard Borich Archives.

Thank you to my brother Jeffrey for modeling for early Ijon Tichy character studies.

My family, Adelaine, Molly, Leo, and Nikolai, for their enthusiasm.

And Bonnie, my eternal flame, my perfect wife.